Not Only War

VICTOR DALY

Not Only War

A STORY OF TWO GREAT CONFLICTS

With an introduction by David A. Davis

With stories from the Crisis

UNIVERSITY OF VIRGINIA PRESS
CHARLOTTESVILLE AND LONDON

Originally published by the Christopher Publishing House in 1932.

University of Virginia Press
Introduction © 2010 by the Rector and Visitors
of the University of Virginia
Printed in the United States of America on acid-free paper

First published 2010

9 8 7 6 5 4 3 2 1

LIBRARY OF CONGRESS CATALOGING-IN-PUBLICATION DATA
Daly, Victor.
  Not only war : a story of two great conflicts / Victor Daly ; with an introduction by David A. Davis.
      p.   cm.
  ISBN 978-0-8139-2971-2 (pbk. : alk. paper)
  1. World War, 1914–1918—Fiction. 2. World War, 1914–1918—Participation, African American—Fiction. I. Title.
  PS3507.A475N67 2010
  813'.52—dc22

                                          2009048702

Frontispiece: Victor Daly in uniform, ca. 1917. (Courtesy of the Division of Rare and Manuscript Collections, Cornell University Library)

Contents

Colored pencil sketch of the 367th Infantry Regiment's insignia, signed by
Victor Daly. (Courtesy of the Division of Rare and Manuscript Collections,
Cornell University Library)

Introduction

DAVID A. DAVIS

Victor Daly's *Not Only War: A Story of Two Great Conflicts*
is the only World War I novel written by an African American veteran. Published in 1932, it received relatively little
attention from the mainstream literary establishment and
faded into obscurity until it, along with many other African
American literary works, was reprinted in the late 1960s.
But even as many other African American texts found
new audiences, *Not Only War* languished. While research-
ing African American World War I literature, I came across
the book in the dusty recesses of a university library, and
I found its portrayal of African American soldiers battling
both German troops and American discrimination compel-
ling. Some exploration into the book's history revealed that
the author's personal story lent interest and credibility to
that of the novel. This, I knew, was an important book.

Recently, several historians and literary scholars have
shed new light on the experience of African American soldiers in World War I.[1] These soldiers laid the groundwork
for the modern civil rights movement, both by demon-
strating the depth of black patriotism and by resisting a
nation that denied their citizenship. Some African American writers of the 1920s and 1930s used black soldiers as
characters to illustrate the inherent contradiction of black
skin and American identity. These stories frequently end
tragically, with the heroic soldier sacrificing himself for a
combination of racial and nationalist reasons. This theme
of duty and sacrifice resonates loudly in *Not Only War*. If

any work makes a case for African American citizenship through military service, then *Not Only War* is it.

Because the book's author is black and because it concerns the color line, the fact that it received no attention in mainstream literary circles is not surprising. No major newspapers reviewed the book, and though a few African American writers such as Langston Hughes traveled in fashionable white artistic circles, Victor Daly gained no significant fame among the white intelligentsia. This reception might be considered irrelevant, since the book was intended specifically for an African American audience, but the response was mixed even among black critics. W. E. B. Du Bois, who published Daly's short stories in the *Crisis*, gave it a brief mention in an omnibus review.[2] Alain Locke, editor of the highly influential anthology *The New Negro*, dismissed it as lacking "the conviction necessary to good fiction" in an annual review of African American literature in 1932.[3] Locke's criticism seems both unwarranted and curious. Although the book does have some melodramatic aspects, it addresses crucial issues of black life in America. Perhaps by the time the book appeared, well more than ten years after the war and near the end of the period known as the Harlem Renaissance, the primary concerns of the African American community had shifted somewhat so that the image of the sacrificial black soldier had become passé. Even so, *Not Only War* explores the social construction of the color line, its obvious sexual connotations, and its less obvious international contradictions as powerfully and with as much conviction as any novel. Daly's credibility as both an African American soldier and as a race man amplifies the book's social and historical significance.

Now that we can reconsider the book and its social context through the long lens of history, the time has come to read and reassess *Not Only War*. As an artifact of a pivotal yet often overlooked period in African American history, *Not Only War* is important as a personal account, as a historical document, and as a work of literature.

Victor Daly: Soldier and Race Man

At the beginning of the twentieth century, before the Great Migration began, a small African American middle class existed in large northern cities. Not all blacks in the North lived comfortably, of course, but the black northern professional class suffered relatively few of the privations and indignities associated with segregation in the South. Many of them led fairly ordinary middle-class lives, in which they lived with, mixed with, attended schools with, and worked with white people. Some, such as W. E. B. Du Bois and Adam Clayton Powell, devoted their careers to securing civil rights for all African Americans. Du Bois labeled this group of educated and advantaged people "the talented tenth" and called upon them to be the vanguard for racial integration in America. In a period when nearly 90 percent of African Americans lived impoverished lives in the South, the northern black bourgeoisie played a crucial social role because their success undercut the white supremacists' ideology of racial inferiority.

Victor Daly grew up in this milieu. Born in New York City on November 22, 1895, he attended integrated public schools. His teachers encouraged him to write, and he won several essay prizes as a high school student. He matriculated at Cornell University, where he joined Alpha Phi Alpha, the nation's first African American fraternity, which began at Cornell in 1905. Attending an Ivy League university and joining the most prominent African American fraternity aligned Daly with the black elite of his generation. Yet he understood, and personally felt, the impact of racial discrimination. Although he had hoped to study journalism, for example, he decided against it because he saw few opportunities for black reporters. Nevertheless, photos from his college scrapbook show ordinary scenes of student life at Cornell: friends at a track meet, tranquil scenes of waterfalls and Lake Cayuaga, and pretty girls in prim outfits.[4] With the exception of his limited career options, Daly seems to have experienced few of the serious hardships most African Americans faced.

When America entered the Great War in Europe, Daly interrupted his education to join the war effort. Thousands of other young men did the same, most out of a sense of patriotism and a desire for glory and adventure. Many African American men felt these urges, but for them racism significantly complicated the issue. Daly saw the war both as an opportunity for adventure and as a means to support the movement for racial equality. Because of his athletic ability and his Ivy League education, he was selected to join a small group of candidates who qualified for the segregated black officers' training camp at Fort Des Moines, Iowa. For him, training was largely an extension of college because the officer cadets tended to form cliques based on their undergraduate schools. Daly wrote exuberant letters back to his fraternity brothers from camp telling them, for example, that "the spirit that exists between the white & colored troops is A#1, they mingle freely and exchange mutual help to an almost amazing degree."[5] This racial harmony may have been the case in specific instances, but most accounts of the officers' training camp and of the African American military experience in general indicate that black soldiers encountered serious discrimination. Of the more than 1200 candidates who entered Fort Des Moines, only 639 graduated, and the majority of black officers were stripped of their command before embarking for France. Daly's experience was exceptional not only in that he saw instances of interracial solidarity in the ranks but also in that he successfully completed the program.

His experience was also exceptional in that he saw active combat. The vast majority of African American soldiers, both officers and enlisted, spent the war in labor battalions, but Daly was assigned to the 367th Infantry Regiment, the Buffaloes. His regiment sailed to France in the summer of 1918 and moved to the front lines in August. In September they joined the Allies' final offensive through the Argonne forest, where they encountered fierce combat. Their moment of greatest glory came on November 10, the day before the armistice, when the regiment rescued an American and a French unit under heavy fire. In gratitude, the French army awarded the entire regiment the Croix de Guerre. On February 24, 1919, Daly returned to America a decorated war hero, and his unit marched triumphantly through Harlem to a hero's welcome.

After returning to the United States, Daly finished his degree, married his college sweetheart, and moved to New York City, where he lived next door to James Weldon Johnson. In 1921 he won a discrimination lawsuit against the Pig and Whistle restaurant, which had refused him, his wife, and his mother-in-law service. He worked for the radical newspaper the *Messenger* briefly before moving to Washington, D.C., in 1922 to work with Dr. Carter G. Woodson on the *Journal of Negro History*.[6] While working there, he contributed short essays to African American periodicals, published three short stories in the *Crisis*, which are reprinted here, and wrote the novel *Not Only War*. In 1934, he joined the U.S. Department of Labor, where he worked to integrate retail stores and transportation systems. He received the department's highest service commendation in 1956 and retired ten years later.[7] He died on May 7, 1986.

Daly devoted his life to securing civil rights for African Americans. In an era when the black bourgeoisie led the fight, he served in trenches, both literally and figuratively. Hundreds of other people worked tirelessly for equality in the generation before the civil rights movement, and as John Egerton explains in *Speak Now against the Day*, their contributions are often overlooked.[8] Daly's novel tells an important story about the African American experience in World War I, but the book itself marks the struggle for civil rights before the movement.

The Story of Two Great Conflicts

Not Only War is the story of two southern soldiers separated by the color line who come together through circumstances beyond their control. Daly had never been to the South when he wrote the book, but he understood—perhaps as a result of his journalistic work with the *Messenger* and the *Journal of Negro History*—that this was the essential site of the African American experience. Harlem may have been in vogue in the 1920s and 1930s, but the majority of blacks still lived in the South, and most of those living in the North had recently migrated from the South, so nearly all African Americans understood the conditions of southern segregation. The color line greatly impacted life in the North, too, but its effects were more obvious in the South.

The book begins with a pair of young southerners eager to enlist for the American Expeditionary Force. The first is Robert Lee Casper, the scion of a prominent upcountry South Carolina planting family. His name reeks of Lost Cause ideology, and Daly characterizes him as a stereotype of white southern values, "a true southerner" (8).[9] He is "faithful to his creed. He believed in the Baptist Church, the supremacy of the white race and the righteousness of the Democratic Party" (8). The other young southerner is the book's protagonist, Montgomery Jason, an idealistic African American college student invested in racial advancement. He sees the war as an opportunity for African Americans to demonstrate their patriotism and to earn social equality.

These two characters represent contending forces in the South during World War I. When the war began, most white southerners supported the isolationism of the Virginia-born Democratic president Woodrow Wilson, but when events dictated that Wilson change his policy, southerners enlisted in huge numbers. This represents a pivotal moment in southern history because it was the first time since the end of the Civil War that southerners began to identify with their nation over their region.[10] Some, however, clung to racism as an overriding ideological bulwark. Senator James Kimble Vardaman of Mississippi opposed the war on the grounds that black soldiers would be trained to kill white Germans and might transfer their training to killing white Americans after the war.[11]

Black southerners, who had been disfranchised by racist voting bills and stripped of their rights by Jim Crow laws, regarded the war with even more conflicted attitudes. Because their rights as U.S. citizens were limited, many did not feel an obligation to support the war or to serve in the military, a position that Daly portrays in the character of Roscoe Simms, who dismisses it as "a white man's war" (12). In contrast, Montie Jason represents the attitude among many African Americans that the war in Europe was a battlefield in the struggle for civil rights. He thinks that if blacks "roll up their sleeves and plunge into this thing, that the Government will reward the race for its loyalty" (12). Naïve though his rhetoric sounds in retrospect, many African American leaders, including W. E. B. Du Bois, held the same conviction.

Du Bois, in fact, wrote a controversial editorial in the *Crisis* that supported the war. "Let us not hesitate," he wrote. "Let us, while this war lasts, forget our special grievances and close our ranks shoulder to shoulder with our own white fellow citizens and the allied nations that are fighting for democracy. We make no ordinary sacrifice, but we make it gladly and willingly with our eyes lifted to the hills."[12] Du Bois hoped that African American involvement in the war would dissolve the color line, and Daly uses Montie's character to explore this hope. However, many other African American leaders supported isolationism, preferring to allow European colonial powers to quarrel amongst themselves. The war's connection to African Americans was not clearly evident, so some black people viewed Du Bois's position skeptically.

Daly's novel is about war, but it is not precisely about World War I. Daly gave the book the extended title *Not Only War: A Story of Two Great Conflicts* because, as he explains in the book's foreward, he believed that African Americans were already involved in a war against the color line. The difference between the wars, he notes, is the battlefield. He employs Sherman's famous declaration that war is hell to describe "physical" combat involving "rapine, destruction and death," but he contends that black people are "born or unconsciously sucked" into a different, psychological hell, "a purgatory for the mind, for the spirit, for the soul of men." By foregrounding this belief, Daly makes the book's political agenda clear: Montgomery Jason is a soldier fighting both against the Germans and against social inequality. In some respects, fighting the Germans is an easier task.

The color line is a more difficult enemy because, to a black southerner, it is omnipresent and omnipotent. Daly illustrates the construction of the color line in the South through the character Miriam Pinckney, a mixed-race schoolteacher. She has attended school in the North, where she has developed notions about racial equality. However, when she returns to the South, she realizes that the color line determines much of her life. Her character alludes to the tragic mullata, a common figure in African American literature. Often the child of a white man and a black woman, the mixed-race character usually suffers rejection from both races, sometimes with fatal consequences, as in the case of William Wells Brown's *Clotel*.[13] In that book, the title character becomes the concubine for a white slaveholder and is eventually dispossessed and drowns herself within sight of the U.S. Capitol. Miriam's fate is less tragic, but she plays a similar role in the text because her own racial composition illustrates that some types of racial mixing are tolerated even under the color line—specifically sexual contact between white men and black women. In Spartanburg, she dates both Montgomery Jason and Robert Casper. Montie clearly harbors romantic feelings for her, perhaps even thoughts of marriage, but Bob, although he admires her, limits their relationship to sex. Miriam deviates from the usual tragic mullata trope because she plays a complicit role in this arrangement. She understands that "southern white men . . . could only seek friendship with comely colored girls for one purpose—a social equality that existed after dark" (26).

The color line in the South had a number of functions: to inculcate an ideology of white supremacy, to maintain a large exploitable labor force, to preserve white political power, and to sustain the purity of the white race. Prohibitions on sexual contact, obviously, did not apply to white men, but black men could be—and frequently were—punished for any sexual contact with white women. Transgressions of the color line could lead to arbitrary acts of racial violence, including lynching. The most common justification for lynching, as Joel Williamson explains, was the accusation of a black man molesting a white woman—a scene that plays out in *The Birth of a Nation*.[14] According to records from Tuskegee Institute, 3,437 African Americans were lynched between 1882 and 1951.[15] The prospect of racial violence loomed over the lives of black people in the United States, and this subtext clearly informs *Not Only War*. The implication behind the book's title and Daly's claim about psychological warfare is that racial violence in the South is as dehumanizing and traumatizing as violence on the battlefields in Europe.

The color line was a serious complication for African American soldiers serving with the American Expeditionary Force in Europe. The U.S. Army formed segregated units specifically designed to replicate the conditions of the Jim Crow South by keeping black men out of positions of authority and away from white women. However, England, France, and Belgium, the countries where the majority of African American soldiers served, did not practice segregation, making egalitarian contact between the

races possible. The army circulated a memo to the French
government that described their fear that "indulgence and
familiarity" between French citizens and black soldiers
would "inspire in black Americans aspirations which to
them [the whites] appear intolerable." It explains that "although a citizen of the United States[,] the black man is
regarded by the white Americans as an inferior being with
whom relations of business or service only are possible,"
and it lists several recommendations for proper conduct
between the races. French soldiers should not, for example, eat with black soldiers, shake hands with them, or
praise them in the presence of white soldiers.[16] The American military command did not intend that the war to save
democracy would lead to equality for black Americans,
even those who served in Europe. But, although the War
Department attempted to replicate segregation in Europe, black soldiers did experience a relative degree of social equality, especially among civilian populations. Addie
Hunton and Kathryn Johnson, who were the only African
American YMCA hostesses in Europe, contend that many
black soldiers "learned that there is a fair-skinned people
in the world who believe in the equality of the races."[17]

Military service in Europe led many African American
soldiers to question their nationalism, as does Montgomery Jason. At one point in the story an old French woman
describes him as "Un Noir, . . . un Americain," and he
thinks to himself, "The world over . . . a nigger first—
an American afterwards" (50). On one level, his realization
indicates a sense of frustration and disillusionment at the
fact that his racial identity overrides his national identity.
On another level, however, his realization opens the possibility for a transnational black identity. In *The Practice
of Diaspora*, Brent Hayes Edwards explains that during
the war African Americans came into contact with French
colonial soldiers from Senegal, Sudan, and the Caribbean
islands and that this contact through military experience
helped forge a culture of black internationalism.[18] Daly

does not explore this aspect of black military service, but he does imply that the experience of living outside the United States changed black soldiers' attitudes toward nationalism and their identities as Americans. Living in Europe gave many black American soldiers—most of whom came from rural, provincial backgrounds—a sense of cosmopolitan sophistication, which directly contributed to their postwar defiance of the color line in the United States.

The War Department especially feared sexual familiarity between French women and black soldiers, a situation that threatened to explode the color line. In a scenario that intentionally mirrors the interracial love triangle in South Carolina, Montgomery Jason meets Blanche Aubertin, an attractive French woman, and, in spite of his deeply ingrained self-protective avoidance of white women, they begin a relationship. He teaches her English, and she asks him difficult questions about race and America:

> Montie had a great deal of difficulty in making her understand that South Carolina was just as much a part of the continental United States, as Normandy was a part of France. Then she wanted to know why he was light brown in color, and had soft, wavy, black hair, while the other sergeants were all black with funny, crinkly hair. Montie was amused at this; but he realized that the amusement was not due to the question itself, but to his own inability to answer it. She was so naïve. (54)

Her questions uncover a number of complex issues relating to the color line, including geographic distinctions, race mixing, and color hierarchy, and the issues themselves are subtly nuanced. Only a lifetime of experience explains the mores of survival in segregated America.

Montie and Blanche's relationship establishes a version of black masculinity that is impossible in the segregated United States. The fact that Montie initially avoids contact with Blanche indicates a diminished sense of masculinity, an essential survival skill in the Jim Crow South. Crossing the color line sexually, the greatest taboo in the South, suggested a new form of potent African American identity, one that transcended nationalism. After the war, Daly commented in the radical newspaper *The Messenger* that "over one thousand Negro stevedores intermarried with white French girls and I doubt if French honor suffered in any way for it."[19] The war exploded the arbitrary connection between nationalism and the color line. If the book ended with Montie marrying Blanche then it might be read as suggesting that the new form of empowered black identity would emerge in Europe, but that is not the case. Bob, who has come to meet Blanche on behalf of a drunken friend, finds her with Montie, and he is outraged at this perceived violation of the color line. He insults Montie and has him tried before a court-martial—on unspecified charges.

The court-martial merely strips Montie of his rank, but a southern mob would have lynched him on precisely the same pretext, a point that both Montie and Bob fully understand. Any shred of idealism about racial equality Montie brought into the military disappears as he realizes that the rationalizations for war—"to make the world safe for democracy—war to end war—self determination for oppressed peoples"—do not apply to black soldiers. "But they don't mean black people," he thinks. "Oh no, black people don't count. They only count the dead" (61). This moment of disillusionment is crucial in the novel because it illustrates the false promise of black military service. Daly deliberately contrives to delay this realization to the last possible moment because the tension between Montie's idealism and the reader's painful awareness of his naïveté drives the narrative.

The Germans attack soon after the court-martial, forcing all soldiers in the vicinity into the trenches. In a highly melodramatic scene, Montie finds Bob mortally wounded, and he faces a serious dilemma: should he kill Bob out of anger and retribution or should he comfort him out of sympathy and humanity? Montie's response, of course, is a foregone conclusion. He sacrifices himself attempting to rescue Bob, and all that remains of them after the attack is their mingled, mangled bodies. Although this ending seems overly sentimental, Mark Whalan documents in *The Great War and the Culture of the New Negro* that this scenario plays out in several African American portrayals of the war. Whalan theorizes that no-man's-land—the territory between the trenches—represents the only raceless, nationless space where actual equality can be realized and where humanity can be achieved, but only when both white and black soldiers face imminent death.[20] The ideology of the color line is so deeply ingrained that only extreme experiences can overcome it.

Jennifer James explains in *A Freedom Bought with Blood* that African American war literature is usually about something other than the actual war.[21] Any depiction of the black body in the uniform of the United States, she argues, is an inherently political act that makes a case for African American citizenship. Many African American writers used the military battlefield as a metaphor for the social battlefield, but what makes Daly's novel especially important as a work of African American war literature is its authenticity. As a war veteran and as an active agent in the early movement for civil rights, he clearly brought to the text a social and artistic agenda. *Not Only War* documents the experience of black soldiers during the war, it depicts the struggle of one individual for self-respect, and it exposes the injustice of the color line on an international scale.

World War I and Black Americans

World War I changed many aspects of American society, including race relations. The war propelled the isolationist United States into international affairs, galvanized the population against a foreign enemy, and caused the first full-scale mobilization and military draft since the end of the Civil War. The war to save democracy in Europe caused several unexpected revolutions in America, including the passage of the women's suffrage amendment, a postwar economic boom, and the Great Migration of African Americans from the South to the North. Submarine warfare in the Atlantic ended the flow of European immigrants into northeastern cities, and the concurrent demand for industrial output to produce war material created an enormous labor market. African Americans in the South, facing racial violence, limited employment opportunities, and the oppressive culture of segregation, moved into northern manufacturing centers, such as Detroit, Chicago, and New York, in huge numbers, and the demographic flow continued until the Great Depression.[22] This population movement, coupled with the social significance of African Americans in uniform, promised to radically change the conditions of African American life in the United States.

While African Americans were evidently willing to leave the South to find work in the North, many were more dubious about actively joining the war effort. In *The Unknown Soldiers: Black American Troops in World War I*, Arthur Barbeau and Henri Florette explain that the prospect of conscripting black soldiers presented the War Department with a serious problem.[23] Many African Americans were ambivalent about America's involvement in the war, but the War Department needed African American enlistment to provide the labor essential to mobilize an expeditionary army. Joel Spingarn and W. E. B. Du Bois, the leaders of the NAACP, saw African American involvement in the war as a means to secure social equality, so they negotiated with the War Department for certain concessions in exchange for their public endorsement. The War Department agreed to draft black and white soldiers proportionally, to outfit African American combat units, and to train black officers, but over time it systematically vacated the arrangement.

Daly was among the relatively small number of African American enlistees who trained for combat leadership roles. Even among those who were admitted to the officer's training camp at Fort Des Moines, most never saw combat. The army, in fact, subscribed to the notion that white southerners understood how best to command blacks, so racist southern officers, similar to Lieutenant Casper, led most black units, which greatly undercut the possibility of military service leading to social equality. No black soldier advanced beyond the rank of colonel, and the army summarily discharged its highest ranking black officer, Col. Charles Young, at the beginning of the war.

Although only a small number of black officers led combat units, the army did field two African American combat divisions. The experience of the Ninety-third Division made perhaps the most credible case for racial equality through military service. General Pershing assigned the Ninety-third, a unit composed partially of well-trained New York National Guard soldiers, to French command, where they served alongside Senegalese troops. The French officers treated the black Americans as equals, and the unit served with distinction. In particular, the 369th Regiment, nicknamed "Harlem's Hellfighters," was commended for serving several weeks in the trenches and repelling multiple German offensives.[24] One soldier in the regiment, Cpl. Henry Johnson, repelled a German raiding party armed with only a pistol and a knife. He killed several Germans, evaded capture, and seized a stockpile of German weapons. He earned the Croix de Guerre and promotion to sergeant, and he became the most famous African American war hero.

The other African American combat unit, however, served under American command and, consequently, earned significantly less recognition. The Ninety-second Division's white commanding officers deliberately sabotaged the unit by assigning them to dangerous missions for which they were untrained and poorly equipped. During the Meuse-Argonne campaign in September 1918, the division failed to occupy a crucial gap between American and French lines. Military officials, including the division's commanding officer, Lt. Gen. Robert Bullard, regarded the failure as a sign of African American soldiers' inherent inferiority. For the remainder of the campaign the division was confined to patrol duties, although some units, including Victor Daly's regiment, distinguished themselves for bravery during the war's final engagements.

Nonetheless, stories of black officers and combat units are highly unusual because the majority of African American soldiers served in labor battalions, euphemistically called the "Services of Supply." More than one hundred and sixty thousand black soldiers—in excess of 70 percent of black enlistment—worked as laborers in uniform. They built camps, loaded and unloaded ships, dug trenches, buried bodies, and performed many of the other menial, degrading, and essential tasks for the army. The army actively recruited white southerners with experience supervising black laborers, such as turpentine and sawmill bosses, chain-gang guards, and farm overseers, to serve as noncommissioned officers in labor battalions. For most black soldiers, therefore, the conditions of life in the military merely extended the conditions of life in the segregated South.

This arrangement was not accidental. Most military commanders believed that black soldiers were unreliable in combat situations and that they were naturally suited to manual labor. They also believed that black laborers would free more white soldiers for combat duty and that limiting black soldiers to labor battalions would mollify white southerners concerned about the presumed danger of combat-trained black veterans. Col. E. D. Anderson, the officer charged with placing black soldiers, wrote in a memo titled "Disposal of the Colored Drafted Men" that he intentionally modeled labor battalions on southern chain gangs. "Each southern state," he wrote, "had negroes in blue overalls working throughout the state with a pick and shovel. When these colored men are drafted they are put in blue overalls (fatigue clothes) and continue to do work with a pick and shovel in the same state where they were previously working."[25] If African Americans imagined military service in World War I as a means toward securing social equality, the War Department deliberately and consistently opposed that agenda.

Inevitably, escalating racial tensions during the war led to violence. The first outbreak occurred in August of 1917, before soldiers were even mobilized, when police officers in Houston, Texas, beat a black soldier. One hundred and fifty armed soldiers marched on the town. Fifteen civilians and four soldiers died in a short skirmish, and the army executed fourteen soldiers.[26] This incident greatly increased public concerns about armed black soldiers. Another violent incident earlier that year in East St. Louis involving black laborers had already aggravated white anxiety. The War Department struggled to maintain racial decorum afterward, especially when black soldiers were stationed in the South. In October 1917 another riot nearly took place in Spartanburg, South Carolina. A white hotel owner hit a black soldier, and black soldiers nearby threatened to attack the hotel, but a black officer, James Europe, restored order.[27] Nonetheless, tensions between white southerners and black soldiers in the area remained high, so the War Department shipped the unit overseas earlier than initially planned. The fact that Daly set *Not Only War* in Spartanburg and used characters from the area may allude directly to this racial tension. The novel mentions "numerous petty clashes with the townspeople and soldiers," but no actual violence occurs in the text (38).

Racial tensions in America escalated after the war, but postwar violence had a distinct difference. Black soldiers returning from Europe, whether they served in combat units or labor battalions, expected a degree of respect, so when attacked by white people, they fought back. Du Bois sounded a militant tone in an editorial in the *Crisis* that clearly indicated that the time for interracial solidarity had passed:

> This is the country to which we Soldiers of Democracy return. This is the fatherland for which we fought! But it is *our* fatherland. . . . We are cowards or jackasses if now that that war is over, we do not marshal every ounce of our brain and brawn to fight a sterner, longer, more unbending battle against the forces of hell in our own land.
>
> We *return.*
>
> We *return from fighting.*
>
> We *return fighting.*
>
> Make way for Democracy! We saved it in France, and by the Great Jehovah, we will save it in the United States of America, or know the reason why.[28]

Du Bois stops just short of advocating open revolt, but his words proved to be prophetic.

During the "Red Summer" of 1919 at least twenty-five race riots erupted around the country. The riots frequently involved either labor tension as white workers attempted to displace black workers or racial tension as black veterans refused to submit to Jim Crow laws.[29] The worst riot happened in Chicago. Although the city had been racially harmonious before the war, thousands of African Americans had arrived from the South during the Great Migration, and by the end of the war segregated housing had begun to appear. In July a fight broke out between black and white Chicagoans at a segregated beach on Lake Michigan. The fighting escalated into a rampage of murder, arson, and looting that lasted for nearly a week, leaving thirty-eight people dead, more than five hundred injured, and more than one thousand homeless. Other riots took place in Pennsylvania, Texas, Arkansas, Georgia, and Washington, D.C. In addition to riots, the number of lynchings, which had fallen somewhat during the war, spiked significantly. More than a dozen African American soldiers were lynched in their uniforms.[30]

In the decade after the war, American society continued to change in tremendous ways. America became a major global diplomatic and economic entity, social values turned more conservative, and women gained political power. The nation enjoyed prosperity but also suffered major upheaval. *Not Only War* reflects these changes by looking back on the prewar condition of African Americans, women, and the nation as a whole from a postwar perspective. At the time Daly published the book in 1932, many of the social issues related to the war had come to a problematic juncture. The Great Depression brought America's prosperity to an end, and the rise of fascism in Europe threatened America's international influence. Meanwhile, in the summer of 1932 more than seventeen thousand disgruntled World War I veterans marched on Washington to demand war service bonuses that Congress had deferred. Active duty soldiers under the leadership of Gen. Douglas MacArthur attacked the veterans, and the image of the U.S. Army attacking its own veterans created a public relations nightmare, which ultimately led to the expansion of the Veterans Administration.[31]

Many of these issues—African Americans in the American Expeditionary Force, the Red Summer, and the march of the Bonus Army—would have resonated in the imaginations of readers coming to *Not Only War* in 1932. Understanding the book's historical context enriches its meaning for today's readers as well. However, though Daly clearly presses a social agenda in the novel by making a case for racial equality, the book has a significance that extends beyond its historical context. It is a critical contribution to the body of American World War I literature.

World War I and the Harlem Renaissance

World War I had a profound impact on American literature. By the time the war began in 1914, the United States
had developed a distinct national culture, but European
culture, because of its tradition and longevity, overshad-
owed America on the international stage. American writers were keenly aware of their provincialism, and the generation of writers coming of age when America entered
the war seized the opportunity to expand their range of
experience and influence. Some joined the army, and others served as war correspondents, as relief workers, or as
ambulance drivers.[32] After the war many American writers congregated in Paris and other European cities, where
they exchanged ideas with foreign writers and artists and
cultivated a new, frequently experimental form of writing
that reflected both recent innovations in the visual arts
and broader social currents. Their books and poems portray world weary, cosmopolitan protagonists struggling
with both individual and collective trauma. Ernest Hemingway's novel *A Farewell to Arms*, the story of an American ambulance driver's tragic romance with an English
nurse near the Italian front lines, epitomizes the dominant
themes of American World War I literature.

African American writers are often placed at the periph-
ery of American World War I literature, but the war directly impacted their work. In fact, in *When Harlem Was
in Vogue*, literary historian David Levering Lewis dates
the beginning of the Harlem Renaissance to February 17,
1919, the day that the 369th Infantry Regiment, "Harlem's
Hellfighters," marched triumphantly through New York
City.[33] By this time the Great Migration had concentrated
African American population in several northern cities,
including New York. The cities themselves were crucial
to the process of developing African American literature
because they allowed black artists—who were previously
dispersed throughout the nation, especially in the South—

to generate a cosmopolitan base of experience. While white writers of World War I literature wrote about the traumas of war, black writers of the Harlem Renaissance wrote about the traumas of both war and racism. So the literature of this period—both black and white—had several important points of congruence, specifically in the experiences of cosmopolitanism and trauma.

Black writers and intellectuals in the cities pressed an active agenda of social change through cultural production, and the sight of proud black soldiers—in spite of the treatment they endured in the army—inspired a more confrontational tone in their works. Claude McKay's 1919 poem "If We Must Die," for example, exhorts black men to "nobly die" while fighting back against their attackers.[34] Black intellectuals created a new racial identity that Alain Locke called the New Negro.[35] An independent black middle class in the cities spawned civic leaders, businessmen, and professionals eager both to pursue social advancement and to promote a more positive, or at least more defiant, image of blackness in the American imagination. In the mid-1920s McKay and James Weldon Johnson were prominent voices for the African American experience, and the publication of Jean Toomer's experimental collection *Cane* in 1923 marked the intersection of black writing and high modernism. By the end of the decade, African American writing enjoyed a new vogue, especially among sophisticated, intellectual circles on both sides of the Atlantic, and Langston Hughes, Zora Neale Hurston, and Wallace Thurman pressed black writing in increasingly ambitious new directions.[36]

The war plays a significant role in the literature of the Harlem Renaissance, but while many white writers depicted the experience of combat whether or not they themselves had actually fought, most black writers deferred their portrayal of combat. Instead, most African American texts of the war focus on African American soldiers reintegrating with life in the United States after the war. There

[handwritten margin notes: "★ this doesn't feel right to me.", "or at least not compl—", "probl— etc.", "re— Am—", "not abroad"]

are at least two likely reasons for this. First, for most black soldiers the actual fighting for freedom, democracy, and self-determination took place in America, not in Europe. Second, very few, if any, black writers other than Victor Daly had actual experience in combat. In most cases, this focus on the home front is entirely appropriate because the more crucial issue from the perspective of the New Negro involved race. Thus, as James and Whalan both argue, black soldiers in literary texts serve a special symbolic purpose to make a case for racial equality through military service.

Jesse Redmon Fauset ventured briefly into the figurative battlefield in *There is Confusion* (1924) in a subplot about a black soldier named Peter Bye.[37] The primary plot of the novel concerns two interrelated families, one black and one white, and the book sprawls over several generations. Aboard a troop ship to France, Peter Bye meets Meriwether Bye, with whom he shares a white ancestor. Their paths cross again in no man's land when Meriwether is mortally wounded and Peter drags his body to sanctuary. This scene, which anticipates the climactic scene of *Not Only War*, establishes the men's actual and metaphorical brotherhood. Fauset's novel was one of the first to portray a black soldier, even as a minor character, and was one of few texts to portray black soldiers in active duty.

Perhaps the most controversial depiction of black soldiers comes from the iconoclastic Claude McKay. In *Home to Harlem* (1928), Jake Brown deserts from a labor battalion in France.[38] From there his story follows a picaresque course through the docks of London, the speakeasies of Harlem, and the filthy living quarters of Pullman car porters. Brown's story undercuts the notion of black patriotism and equal citizenship through military service. The story ends with Brown disillusioned and alienated, fleeing the possibility of imprisonment for desertion. Jake Brown reappears in *Banjo* (1929) among a cosmopolitan crew of destitute black dock workers from Europe, Africa, the

West Indies, and the U.S. South in Marseilles, France.[39] This book suggests that race makes for stronger bonds of solidarity than nationality, which places McKay's stories somewhat at odds with most other portrayals of black soldiers.

Black veterans figured prominently in several other postwar African American writings. The protagonist of Walter White's *The Fire in the Flint* (1924) is a doctor who served in France before returning to open a clinic in Georgia.[40] E. C. Williams's epistolary novel, originally serialized in the *Messenger* in 1925 and recently republished as *When Washington Was in Vogue*, tells the story of a bourgeois black scholar and Fort Des Moines officer who chastely romances a black flapper.[41] Veterans appear as minor characters in Nella Larsen's novels *Quicksand* (1928) and *Passing* (1929), in Langston Hughes's *Not Without Laughter* (1930), and in Zora Neale Hurston's *Jonah's Gourd Vine* (1934). They also appeared in numerous short stories, plays, and poems, most frequently in works published between 1925 and the beginning of World War II.[42] Black veterans have appeared in recent works as well. Shadrack, a shell-shocked veteran, invents the National Suicide Day ritual in Toni Morrison's *Sula* (1973), and Rita Dove includes a sequence of poems about black World War I soldiers in her collection *American Smooth* (2004).[43]

Although black veterans populated numerous works published in the 1920s, James Weldon Johnson claimed in 1930 that "the Negro novel of the World War is still unwritten."[44] Black war experience and the defiant attitudes of the New Negro suffused black cultural production at the time, so it is strange that no novel had yet featured a black soldier in active duty as a primary character. To that point, black soldiers had been depicted more as symbols than as characters. *Not Only War* is the African American novel of World War I. It tells the story of black military service that is almost impossible to find elsewhere. In this novel we see the promise of military service as a means to racial equality, we see the complexity of the color line both in America and abroad, we see the effects of French society on black soldiers, we see the disillusionment of black soldiers in the segregated army, and we see the extent of the sacrifice expected from them. Daly brings to the text his authentic experience in both the actual trenches of France and the metaphorical trenches of the race struggle.

Immediately after World War I, black soldiers figured prominently in many literary works, which reflected the role of black soldiers and veterans in American culture. But in the wake of World War II and the civil rights movement, the experience of these soldiers has been largely forgotten. This is unfortunate because the experiences and sacrifices of black soldiers in World War I laid the foundation for the progress that would follow in the second half of the twentieth century. *Not Only War* offers us a means to reconnect with this pivotal moment in American history and to better understand both the physical and the psychological hell of war for black Americans.

NOTES

1. New books on the African American experience in World War I include Richard Slotkin, *Lost Battalions: The Great War and the Crisis of American Nationality* (New York: Henry Holt, 2005) and forthcoming books by Adriane Lentz-Smith, Jennifer Keene, and Chad Williams.

2. W. E. B. Du Bois, "The Browsing Reader," *Crisis* 41.4 (April 1932): 138.

3. Alain Locke, "We Turn to Prose: A Retrospective Review of the Literature for the Negro for 1931," in *The Critical Temper of Alain Locke*, edited by Jeffery C. Stewart (New York: Garland Publishing, 1983), 212.

4. Victor Daly's personal papers, including a scrapbook of his time as a student and as a cadet, are located in the Cornell University Kroch Library Rare and Manuscript Collection.

5. Additional images and information about Daly at Fort Des Moines can be found on the Alpha Phi Alpha fraternity's web exhibit on the Great War: http://rmc.library.cornell.edu/alpha/greatwar/.

6. Daly elided his work on the *Messenger* in his later career, which, considering the paper's Communist agenda, might have been essential to his career in government service.

7. More biographical information on Daly can be found in James Payne's interview with him in this volume. It was originally published in *MELUS* 12.2 (Summer 1985): 87–92.

8. John Egerton, *Speak Now Against the Day: The Generation Before the Civil Rights Movement in the South* (Chapel Hill: University of North Carolina Press, 1995).

9. References to the text of *Not Only War* appear in parentheses.

10. Jeanette Keith, *Rich Man's War, Poor Man's Fight: Race, Class, and Power in the Rural South during the First World War* (Chapel Hill: University of North Carolina Press, 2004).

11. Vardaman's opposition to the war ultimately led to his political defeat. See William F. Holmes, *The White Chief: James Kimble Vardaman* (Baton Rouge: Louisiana State University Press, 1970).

12. W. E. B. Du Bois, "Close Ranks," in *W. E. B. Du Bois: A Reader*, edited by David Levering Lewis (New York: Henry Holt, 1995), 697.

13. William Wells Brown, *Clotel; or, The President's Daughter* ([1853] New York: Penguin, 2003).

14. Joel Williamson, *The Crucible of Race: Black-White Relations in the South since Emancipation* (New York: Oxford University Press, 1984).

15. Detailed records of lynchings can be found in Robert L. Zangrando, *The NAACP Crusade against Lynching, 1909–1950* (Philadelphia: Temple University Press, 1980).

16. W. E. B. Du Bois, "Documents of the War," *Crisis* 18.1 (May 1919): 16–21.

17. Addie W. Hunton and Kathryn M. Johnson, *Two Colored Women with the American Expeditionary Forces* ([1920] New York: G. K. Hall & Co., 1997), 324.

18. Brent Hayes Edwards, *The Practice of Diaspora: Literature, Translation, and the Rise of Black Internationalism* (Cambridge: Harvard University Press, 2003), 3–4.

19. Quoted in Chad Louis Williams, "Torchbearers of Democracy: The First World War and the Figure of the African American Soldier" (Ph.D. Diss., Princeton University, 2004), 268.

20. Mark Whalan discusses the role of no man's land in African American writing in *The Great War and the Culture of the New Negro* (Tallahassee: University Press of Florida, 2008), 69–81.

21. Jennifer C. James, *A Freedom Bought with Blood: African American War Literature from Civil War to World War II* (Chapel Hill: University of North Carolina Press, 2007).

22. See James N. Gregory, *The Southern Diaspora: How the Great Migrations of Black and White Southerners Transformed America* (Chapel Hill: University of North Carolina Press, 2005).

23. Arthur E. Barbeau and Florette Henri, *The Unknown Soldiers: Black American Troops in World War I* (Philadelphia: Temple University Press, 1974). For an engaging contemporary account, see Emmett J. Scott, *Scott's*

Official History of the American Negro in the World War ([1919] New York: Arno Press, 1969).

24. The 369th's fascinating regimental history can be found in Stephen L. Harris, *Harlem's Hell Fighters: The African American 369th Infantry in World War I* (Washington: Potomac Books, 2003).

25. Quoted in Arthur E. Barbeau and Florette Henri, *The Unknown Soldiers: Black American Troops in World War I* (Philadelphia: Temple University Press, 1974), 199.

26. See Robert V. Haynes, *A Night of Violence: The Houston Riot of 1917* (Baton Rouge: Louisiana State University Press, 1976).

27. Richard Slotkin narrates the Spartanburg incident in *Lost Battalions*, 115–23.

28. W. E. B. Du Bois, "Returning Soldiers," in *The Oxford W. E. B. Du Bois Reader*, edited by Eric J. Sundquist (New York: Oxford University Press, 1996), 380–81.

29. See William M. Tuttle, *Race Riot: Chicago in the Red Summer of 1919* (Urbana: University of Illinois Press, 1996).

30. The image of the lynched soldier figured prominently in many African American texts about the war. See David A. Davis, "Not Only War is Hell: World War I and African American Lynching Narratives," *African American Review* 42.3–4 (Fall/Winter 2008): 477–91.

31. More information of the Bonus Army can be found in Paul Dickson and Thomas B. Allen, *The Bonus Army: An American Epic* (New York: Walker and Co., 2005).

32. For background on American World War I literature see Stanley Cooperman, *World War I and the American Novel* (Baltimore: Johns Hopkins University Press, 1970); Keith Gandal, *The Gun and the Pen: Hemingway, Fitzgerald, Faulkner and the Fiction of Mobilization* (New York: Oxford University Press, 2008); and John T. Matthews, "American Writing of the Great War," in *The Cambridge Companion to the Literature of the First World War*, edited by Vincent Sherry (New York: Cambridge University Press, 2005), 217–44.

33. David Levering Lewis, *When Harlem Was in Vogue* (New York: Knopf, 1981), 3.

34. Claude McKay, "If We Must Die," in *Complete Poems*, edited by William J. Maxwell (Urbana: University of Illinois Press, 2004).

35. Alain Locke, ed., *The New Negro* ([1925] New York: Touchstone, 1999).

36. For more information about the Harlem Renaissance, see, in addition to Lewis's *When Harlem Was in Vogue*, Houston Baker, *Modernism and the Harlem Renaissance* (Chicago: University of Chicago Press, 1987) and George Hutchinson, *The Harlem Renaissance in Black and White* (Boston: Belknap, 1995).

37. Jesse Redmon Fauset, *There is Confusion* ([1924] Boston: Northeastern University Press, 1989).

38. Claude McKay, *Home to Harlem* ([1928] Boston: Northeastern University Press, 1987).

39. Claude McKay, *Banjo* ([1929] New York: Harvest, 1970).

40. Walter White, *The Fire in Flint* ([1924] Athens: University of Georgia Press, 1995).

41. Edward Christopher Williams, *When Washington Was in Vogue* (New York: Amistad, 2004).

42. Mark Whalan exhaustively catalogs texts in which black soldiers appear in *The Great War and the Culture of the New Negro*, 45.

43. Toni Morrison, *Sula* (New York: Plume, 1973), and Rita Dove, *American Smooth* (New York: Norton, 2004), 41–70.

44. James Weldon Johnson, *Black Manhattan* ([1930] New York: Atheneum, 1972), 276.

Publisher's Note

Several apparent typographical errors in the original edition of *Not Only War* have been silently corrected in the text. A list of these emendations is below.

Page/line	Original text	Emendation
19/9	they're	there're
33/19	think,"	think?"
43/11	was thunderous	was a thunderous
49/23	the're	there're
55/7	written.	written:
68/6	strength	strengthen

Not Only War

A STORY OF TWO GREAT CONFLICTS

DEDICATED TO THE ARMY OF THE DISILLUSIONED

Foreword

William Tecumseh Sherman branded War for all time when he called it Hell. There is yet another gaping, abysmal Hell into which some of us are actually born or unconsciously sucked. The Hell that Sherman knew was a physical one— of rapine, destruction and death. This other, is a purgatory for the mind, for the spirit, for the soul of men. Not only War is Hell. —The Author

I

Col. Clarke Casper divided his attention between his three-minute eggs and a letter which he held in his left hand.

"Well that's fine," he said as he concluded the letter.

"Good news?" asked his wife.

"What's up, Dad?" questioned his son Bob, looking up from the morning paper.

"Well, it's the end of a long, long fight," replied the Colonel, pushing the empty plates away from him, and going back to his letter. "Ever since I became Chairman of the County School Board ten years ago, I have waged a bitter fight to improve the schools in this county—especially the schools for the Negroes. Conditions have been worse than deplorable, but the petty politicians who have charge of appropriations and expenditures have turned a deaf ear to every plea. Last year I actually had to threaten to resign and expose them, before I could get them to fix a roof on a school shack, that leaked like a sieve."

"I don't see why, at your age Clarke, you don't resign and leave these worries to younger heads, anyhow?" interrupted his wife.

"Well, I suppose I should. But you know that I have led an active life, and I must have something to keep me interested and occupied. I can't devote much time to the plantation any more, and this school business is a good outlet. Besides, since I've gotten into the work, I wanted to stick to it until I could improve these wretched conditions here in the county."

The old Colonel had stood up. He was leaning with his arms resting on the back of his chair. The open letter was still in his hand.

"This letter is the announcement that the county is to have a fine, brand new school for the Negro children next Fall," exultantly continued the Colonel.

"Congratulations, Dad—great work!" said his son with admiration, affectionately slapping the old man's shoulders. "How'd you do it?"

"Through the aid of a fund established by a wealthy man in Chicago for just this purpose," replied his father. "We could have had it long ago, if the county had been willing to do its share. It's been a battle, my boy, but you know how we Caspers fight."

"You deserve a lot of credit, Clarke," complimented his wife, "I know how hard you've worked. Now that you have accomplished something, I do hope that you'll give it up. It's such a worry."

"I couldn't think of it now, dear, at least not until the school has been established and is in good running shape. The whole thing might go to pieces if I were to quit now."

"You've got to take it easy though, Dad, just as Mother says." Bob glanced at his wrist watch. "Hullo! I've got less than an hour to make the 10:15 for Spartanburg," he exclaimed. He skipped out into the great hall of the old mansion and took the flight of stairs two steps at a time.

The stock of which Robert Lee Casper came had two prime factors—it was old, and it was pugnacious. Nobody knew just exactly how the Casper seed had been planted in South Carolina. However, as far back as the Revolution the Caspers had been fighting. Old John Casper had helped make life miserable for the British in the swamps of Carolina with Marion and Sumpter. In return for his service to the Continental cause he had been rewarded with a small tract of arable land that formerly belonged to a Tory family. Old John had therefore, for historical purposes, become number one of the house of Casper, and the small tract of land became the ancestral home. Some generations later, one of John's descendants had named the old homestead "Broad Acres," and erected a fine colonial mansion. When cotton became King, the family fortunes had multiplied. The grandson of rough old John Casper was one of the largest and wealthiest slave-holders in the State and his influence was as broad as his plantations.

When the war broke out in '61, this same Charles Casper of the broad acres, wide influence and many slaves became a colonel of cavalry in the South Carolina militia. He gave freely from his coffers to the lost cause. When the struggle was over he returned home, a broken old man, to find his colonial home in ruins, his plantations laid waste, his slaves gone and the remnants of his family scattered. The Casper spirit of never-say-die was sorely tested through these dark days.

It was left to Clarke, youngest of the Caspers, then barely a lad of sixteen to repair the family fences and fortunes. Through the trying days of Reconstruction, he labored at his task, aided by a few of the faithful freed men, who like himself, had been born and reared on the plantation. Twelve years after the war he rode with Wade Hampton and the "Red Shirts." From then on the Caspers were once more riding the crest. The family had staged its comeback.

This was the heritage that flowed through the veins of young Robert Lee Casper. Educated at one of the South's leading military schools, Bob Casper represented a fine example of young American manhood. The spring of his senior year had seen the outbreak of the war with Germany. Soon followed the War Department's announcement of the establishment of the Officer's Training Camps. True Casper, the announcement was hardly published, before Bob was on his way home to take the physical examination for appointment to one of the Camps. That accounted for his presence at "Broad Acres" the morning that his father had received the letter about the new school.

Bob had lived among colored people all his life. He owed much of his fine athletic body to the start that his mammy had given him. As a little fellow, the only playmates that he knew were the Negro children of the tenant farmers on the plantation. Many an evening he had sat in a deep rocker on the veranda of the big house and listened to the distant strains of a banjo or the crooning voices harmonizing on the old familiar songs. As a matter of fact, he had learned to strum a banjo from one of the Negro boys—and his banjo had been among his chief assets when he went off to college.

But Bob Casper was a true Southerner. The blood of his grandfather and his uncles had not been spilled in vain. He was faithful to his creed. He believed in the Baptist Church, the supremacy of the white race and the righteousness of the Democratic Party.

II

Bob appeared in the great hall again, several minutes later—this time with his traveling bag. He seemed to be running in circles, like a rabbit in a cage.

"But Bob you'll just have to wait and catch a later train," his mother was remonstrating with him.

"You don't understand, Mother, I have a definite engagement with Captain Hendricks this afternoon at the Jackson House. My appointment to Camp may depend on the outcome of that conference."

"Well, why didn't you speak to Rufus last night?"

"But it's all so unusual, Mother! Who would have thought that old Rufus would be going up to town with the carriage and horses before sun-up, and that there wouldn't be a soul here to drive me to the Junction?"

"Why don't you walk down to the road then? Somebody may be going along in your direction and be glad to give you a lift."

"I think I'll do that, Mother. Good-bye. I'll be back some time to-morrow. Tell Dad good-bye for me. So long!"

Bob kissed his mother, picked up his bag and set out at a brisk pace down the gravel walk.

It was a glorious morning. A cool, caressing breeze rustled the leaves in the trees that lined the walk. The rays of the sun, beaming down brightly upon two shapely birches, were so beautifully reflected by the silver gray of the bark and leaves, that it reminded Bob of the refraction of light shining through a prism. Even in his haste, he had to stop for a second look.

Bob Casper was in high spirits. In spite of his temporary annoyance, he felt that somehow he would make that train. The Junction was only three miles down the road, and there were still forty minutes left. One couldn't be pessimistic on a morning like this. And as for the Training Camp? He just had to be appointed. But, he cautioned himself, there were thousands of fellows who felt the same way. The competition would be keen. That was why he wanted to see Hendricks. Hendricks could fix it if he wanted to. Oh, he'd fix it all right. One couldn't be pessimistic on a morning like this.

But in spite of his optimism, the only living thing that Bob could find on the road was an under-sized chip-munk, that made periodic excursions into and out of the old stone wall across the road from where Bob was standing.

"Even if a buggy does come along now, I'll hardly make it," he murmured to himself, impatiently looking at his watch for the hundredth time. "Guess I'm licked. I'll have to take the afternoon train," he concluded bitterly.

He turned to enter the gate, and then stopped short and wheeled about as though suddenly charged with electricity. He cupped his ear.

"Yep, it's a horse!" he cried, running out into the center of the road to get a better view. The quick steps were clearly audible now coming around the bend in the road.

"By George, a buggy!" he exclaimed—and then his heart

sank. It was only a small two-seated gig, and it was occupied by a couple of colored girls. When they saw Bob
standing in the middle of the road, the one who was driving reined in, and the horse slowed down to a walk.

"I thought you were going to the Junction," explained
Bob, visibly disappointed, as he moved out of the way of
the vehicle.

"We are," replied the girl who was driving.

"And we're terribly late," put in her companion. Bob noticed a small hand bag in her lap—and that she was un-
commonly pretty. "We're trying to make the 10:15."

"So was I," he replied.

"Aren't you still trying to make it?" questioned the one
with the bag.

Bob thought that he could detect the faintest flash of an
amused smile across the pretty face.

"Well, you see—I thought—perhaps—oh well, it's too
late now, anyway. You all will have to hurry or you'll miss
it yourselves."

The two girls exchanged glances.

"I wish we could help you," said the one who had done
most of the talking.

"That's all right," he answered. His face was worried,
however.

"If you don't mind driving—and a tight fit—my cousin
here can sit in my lap—and you, why you can make your
train," ventured the pretty one.

The Casper mind flashed into action.

"What! ride down to the Junction beside two niggers!"
he thought. "Hell, I'd rather miss a dozen trains. And she's
got a helluva nerve asking me to ride down there with
them, anyhow. Still she's damned good-looking—and neat
and clean, too. But what would folks think, seeing me driving down to the station with a couple of nigger girls. But
Hell, I may miss Hendricks altogether, and it may cost
me my commission. I've got to go. Damn, but she's got a
pretty face!"

"I wouldn't want to crowd you, but I must make that train," he finally answered, still somewhat hesitantly.

"Oh we don't mind being crowded. It's only a short distance. Climb up."

Not a word was exchanged all the way to the Junction. Bob held his heart in his mouth lest he pass someone whom he knew on the road. Yet he argued with himself, "She's a damned pretty girl, and I'm making my train. Hell, during war-times folks do all sorts of things. It's an emergency of war, that's all."

They arrived at the station, without incident, a few minutes ahead of time. As Bob dismounted from the buggy he glanced about him furtively, to see if anybody in the station was looking at him. The platform was practically deserted, however, and he felt very much relieved.

"I live in the white house on the road where you gave me the lift. The name is R. L. Casper. If I can ever be of service to you, don't hesitate to call on me."

"Thank you, Mr. Casper," replied the pretty one, since he seemed to address all of his remarks to her. "I suppose the full name is Robert Lee Casper."

"How'd you guess it?" enquired the surprised Bob.

"R. L. could hardly mean anything else in the South," she answered with a smile. "But here comes the train. Good-bye, Geneva! I'll drop you a line from Spartanburg. Take good care of Mumsey till I get back. Good-bye, Mr. Casper!"

"But I say, I told you my name and where I lived, you might at least tell me who you are," complained Bob, his curiosity now thoroughly aroused.

"Oh, that's hardly necessary, Mr. Casper, some other time perhaps." And with that same little trace of amusement, she turned and walked rapidly in the direction of the panting locomotive.

III

"You've trumped my ace, you big sap!" wailed Roscoe Simms.

"What of it?" came the laconic reply. "It's not the first ace that's ever been trumped." Montgomery Jason threw his cards on the table, and started to rise, "I'm sick of this game, anyhow," he added.

"You're not quitting, are you Montie?" asked Jim Beasely.

"And breaking up the game?" added Teddy Burwell.

"Aw, come on Montie, pull yourself together and snap out of it. What the devil's wrong with you, anyhow?" continued Simms, looking woefully down upon the ace of hearts, partly obscured by the deuce of clubs.

"How can you fellows sit around all day and half the night playing cards, in times like these?" protested Montie. "Hell, the whole damn world's on fire!"

"Well, I ain't no fireman—I'm only a college boy," modestly explained Beasely.

"There you go again, Montie," wailed Simms, registering the utmost disgust. "All you think about is the war! You know what Sherman said about war. Well, he knew a damn sight more about it than either me or you. Besides, what have we got to do with the war, anyhow? It's a white man's war. He started it. Let him finish it. There's nothing in it for us."

"Not a damn thing!" agreed Burwell.

"Oh, I don't know about that," answered Montie, showing interest for the first time. "I think that if we roll up our sleeves and plunge into this thing, that the Government will reward the race for its loyalty."

"Is that so?" sneered Simms. "I read somewhere that the loyalty of a slave to his master is a vice. No amount of sacrifice on your part or my part, will ever soften the hearts of these crackers toward us. You're just condemned to ride in a Jim Crow car for the rest of your life. Your children will attend Jim Crow schools—war or no war—fight or no fight. You'll live in a segregated neighborhood for the remainder of your days—and they'll lynch you whenever they get ready."

"Well, what's your program?" Montie asked.

"Program!" shouted Simms. "What the devil do I want with a program? I have no program. All I want to do is to finish my college work here, get into a medical school in the North or West, settle down to practice—and tell these crackers where to go."

"But they are not going to let you do that, Big Boy— that's just my point. The war, don't you see? Your career will be altered by it! What if you are drafted—made to serve? What then?" Montie looked at each of his three companions in turn.

"What then?" he demanded again.

Not a soul answered.

"Well, I for one will never wait to be drafted," continued Montie. "The War Department promises to open a Training Camp for colored officers. Just as soon as the announcement is definitely made, I'm going to volunteer for Camp."

"But what makes you think you'd be appointed, Montie," questioned Beasely, "you're just twenty-one; and I understand that the preference is to be given to the older applicants. There's only to be the one Camp, you know, to take care of the ten million of us."

"Well, maybe if enough of us apply, they'll give us a second Camp. Who knows?" replied Montie, undaunted.

"Not a chance," piped up Teddy Burwell, "the way they're hesitating and dilly-dallying about this first Camp proves that. I think they're waiting for the end of the war to help them make a decision, anyhow."

"You fellows mustn't be so darned pessimistic," concluded Montie. "Maybe we'll hear something definite about the Camp before the end of the week. This suspense is awful. Come on, let's take a walk into town, the old burg's full of soldiers—sort of concentration camp, I believe, for the National Guard."

"That's what 'Prof' Holmes was saying this morning," agreed Roscoe Simms. "Let's go."

IV

"Why, Mr. Casper?"

"Just strolled in here to take a smoke. The smoker's too far back. Besides you owe me an apology. So I had a double reason for coming up here."

"An apology?"

"Yes, for running off and leaving me on the station platform without giving me your name."

Bob Casper was smiling down into the pretty face of her-lady-of-the-buggy-ride. Once again he thought that he could detect that flash of a smile that intrigued him so much. He knew that he had no right to be there. In spite of himself he knew that the "emergency of war" had ended with his arrival at the Junction. But he just couldn't get that pretty face off his mind. "And she seemed so lively and bright, too," he thought to himself. There was no comparison between her and any of the Negro women or girls that he had ever seen around the plantations. He had tried unsuccessfully to get her off his mind by reading. But the words meant nothing to him. Then he tried to take a nap. That was even worse. He attempted to rehearse his coming conference with Captain Hendricks. But the thoughts refused to come. "Time enough for that when I get there," he muttered. "Think I'll stroll through to the colored coach and get a smoke. I'll feel better. And what if I do see her and say a few words to her? What harm would it do? Sometimes this damn prejudice seems to have no sense in it at all."

Miriam Pinckney was brown. But her skin must have

been transparent. Somehow, one didn't think of Miriam in terms of common color. She glowed—like burnished gold. As she gazed up in surprise at Bob Casper, her half-open mouth partially exposed two rows of small, even, white teeth. Her hair, black and wavy, was gathered into two large knots over each ear. But it was her eyes that fascinated Bob. They seemed to be smiling all the time—yet they could be serious, he thought. They were eyes that didn't merely look—they seemed to look through, and through, and through. Maybe, he wondered, it was because the lashes were so long, or the brows were so black. Like most men attracted to a pretty face, Bob never noticed her dress. But perhaps, after all, it was not his fault, for the pale yellow organdie with a white sash that Miriam was wearing, was extremely simple. It was very becoming however, and served as a background to complete the picture at which he was gazing. A broad-brimmed straw hat of the same yellow shade rested on the seat beside her.

"What's in a name?" she asked, in answer to his demand for an apology.

"But you have the advantage of me?" he protested.

Miriam ignored his protest. "I·am glad that you were able to make your train. How far are you going?" she asked.

"To Spartanburg; and I'm mighty glad that you happened along when you did. I have a very important engagement there this afternoon. My appointment to camp may depend on it."

"Camp? Are you going off to war?" she questioned in surprise.

He laughed—a pleasant little laugh, she thought.

"Not exactly; at least, not yet," Bob said.

Bob glanced around him. He noticed that the Jim Crow car was comparatively empty. A few drowsy men, most of them in blue denim overalls, were sunken deep into their seats. One man had pushed back the seat in front of him, removed his shoes, and was practically stretched out across the two seats. An open basket with two live chickens, their feet tied together with twine, rested on the seat beside him. Most of the windows were closed to keep out the cinders, because the coach was directly behind the locomotive. A couple of indifferent-looking white men sat together near the door, drawing nonchalantly on a pair of corn-cob pipes, from which there issued at intervals dense clouds of ill-smelling, nauseating smoke.

"It's stuffy in here," complained Bob somewhat embarrassed, and looking about as though hunting for a place to escape. "Must you stay in this?" he finally exploded.

"You know I must," she replied, "but it's not much farther now. How about you? Certainly you can't enjoy standing up in here."

"You have no objection to my being here, have you?" Bob asked quickly.

"Oh, no! None at all! I would ask you to take a seat if conditions were a little more pleasant."

"It would be more comfortable sitting down," he ventured.

With a quick glance at the other passengers, he threw back the seat in front of her, and sat down facing Miriam. He continued to smoke his cigarette. For several minutes neither of them spoke.

"And where are you headed for?" he finally asked.

"Spartanburg."

"Oh yes, I do remember. Is that your home?"

"No," she replied, "I'm only going there to visit a classmate for a couple of weeks. My home is less than a mile from yours."

"What? But—how is it that I have never run into you before?" he blurted out.

They both laughed. Then her manner changed. The laughing eyes became serious.

"You see the schools are so bad here in the State, that my folks have kept me away in boarding school ever since I was old enough to read. I only come home for a few weeks each summer."

"I understand that the school situation is bad. My father is chairman of the County School Board. I have heard him say that it is a constant fight to get sufficient appropriations to keep the schools going, much less to improve them. However, there's to be a fine new school for the colored this Fall. Some fellow from Chicago has donated most of the money."

Miriam's eyes were fairly dancing now.

"Is that so?" she exclaimed. "Then they will need a teacher."

Bob smiled. "You can't have schools without teachers," he said, amused. "Are you interested?"

"Am I interested—interested, did you say? I'm fairly carried away with excitement! If I could get that position, Mr. Casper, in a few years time I could go away and complete my music."

"Oh, are you musical?"

"Not half as much as I want to be. Would you help me to get that job?" She seemed to be trembling with emotion.

"How can I when I don't even know your name!" he teased.

They both laughed again.

"Is that the only condition?" she countered.

"You misunderstood me," he replied to the thrust, "I didn't say that I was the chairman of the County School Board."

"But aren't you your father's son?" she laughed.

"You should study law instead of music," he commented.

"Is that a brick-bat or a bouquet?"

"Take your choice!" he laughed.

"Spartanburg! Spartanburg! All out for Spartanburg!" clamored the train conductor from the platform.

Bob jumped from his seat.

"I must be going," he said, "my bag's two cars back. I had no idea that we were so close in. But say, you haven't given me your name yet!"

"I thought that you had forgotten." She opened her purse and took out a small card and pencil. She scribbled something in one corner, and thrust the card into his hand, as the train pulled into the station.

"Thanks," he cried over his shoulder, as he hurried across the platform to the next car.

As he stood on the car step a few moments later waiting for the train to stop, he glanced down at the card which he still held in his hand, and read.

"Miriam Pinckney" printed in Old English, and scribbled in the corner, "in care of Reed, 39 Vine Street, Spartanburg."

"She'd make a helluva good buddy, if it weren't for this damned race prejudice," he mumbled to himself as he swung off the train.

V

Montgomery Jason and Roscoe Simms had been roommates and buddies for three years. During all that period it was a known fact that they had never agreed on a single subject of major importance. Truly theirs was an attraction of opposites.

"Why didn't the other fellows come along?" asked Montie, as he joined his chum on the path leading from the dormitory down to the gate.

"Beasely says he's got to get off a letter to his old man, or he'll be stranded here; and Teddy Burwell's cramming."

"Cramming! I thought he was through with his exams," said Montie.

"He's taking a make-up in math, I believe," replied Roscoe.

The two friends swung leisurely along the walk and out of the campus gate into the main highway. The sun was still fairly high, and although the sky was cloudless, the day had not been unbearably warm. In fact, a redeeming breeze made the late afternoon ideal for strolling.

According to prediction, as the boys neared the city, the road became more and more crowded with soldiers. Motor trucks clattered hither and thither. Motor-cycles with side-cars darted in and out through the traffic. Important-looking army officers gazed condescendingly from the windows of olive-colored automobiles that sounded imperative horns for the right of way.

"Damn!" exclaimed Roscoe, as they barely cleared a big limousine flying a red flag with two white stars, "there're more soldiers in Spartanburg than a dog has fleas."

"Where'll we go, Roscoe?" enquired Montie several minutes later.

"Oh, I don't know. Anywhere. Let's go by the drug-store and get a soda."

"And an evening paper," added Montie.

The two room-mates bent their steps in the direction of the Negro section of the city. The drug-store graced one of its most prominent corners. In the absence of a community house or a club of any sort, this store served as general meeting place for the younger set. As soon as the heat of the day had passed the young folks sallied forth— the girls to look their prettiest, and the fellows to observe them. The big parade, of course, passed in front of the drug-store, which became a sort of reviewing stand. Groups of the girls, or a pair of couples would drop into the drug-store and take a table at one of the vantage points in the window. As fast as a table became vacant there was always someone waiting to seize it.

When Montie and Roscoe reached the drug-store corner, it was still a little early for the review. The marchers were gathering, but the parade was not yet in full swing.

"Good! We can get a table," remarked Roscoe as they entered.

"Can't sit here all evening drinking one soda," dryly replied his companion.

"What's the matter with taking two or three?"

"You goin' to pay for them?" questioned Montie.

"You're always taking the joy out of life," commented Roscoe as he pulled out a chair and sat down next to the window. "I'm going to time myself and see how long I can make this soda last."

"What do you do? Keep adding water?"

After the clerk had taken the order, Roscoe gave his attention to the strollers outside the window, while Montie glanced over the evening paper.

Suddenly Roscoe grabbed his chum's arm.

"Well, I'll be darned, look who's here!" he exploded to the astonished Montie.

Montie gave one look, dropped the paper and bounded like a kangaroo out of the door.

"Miriam Pinckney! What are you doing here?" he was exclaiming a moment later, taking her by both hands.

"Hello, Montie—this is a surprise! I thought that you would have been gone by now. Meet my friend, Miss Hazel Reed."

"How do you do, Miss Reed? Won't you ladies join us in a little refreshment? There's Roscoe in the drug-store."

"What do you say, Hazel?" asked Miriam. "I want you to meet Roscoe, anyhow; he's a scream."

"Who says I'm a scream?" chirped Roscoe, appearing at the door to welcome the party. "Hello, Miriam, I haven't seen you in a month of Sundays!"

"It's like old times to see you, Roscoe," Miriam replied. "This is my friend Miss Hazel Reed—Mr. Roscoe Simms."

"It's a pleasure to know you, Miss Reed," said Roscoe.

"I've heard Miriam speak of you both so much that I feel as if I've known you for a long time," replied Hazel.

Half an hour later the party had joined the parade. Roscoe was strolling in front with Hazel. Montie and Miriam, arm in arm, were thoroughly absorbed in each other a few paces behind.

"Why didn't you answer my last letter?" Montie asked her.

"It came in the midst of my final exams, and when I did

get ready to answer it, I realized that you must have gone; because you had finished with your own exams when you wrote me. What are you doing here so late, anyway? Aren't you going back to Buckroe this summer?"

Montie shook his head.

"Not if I can help it," he said slowly, "I'm all up in the air. I want to get into an Officers Training Camp. I don't want to be drafted. They're not taking colored into the Camps at present; but they have promised to open a separate camp for colored officers. No details have been announced yet, as to when or where. That's what I'm hanging around here for now. I'd have to come back here to be examined, since I would have to claim residence in this state."

"Somehow I never thought of you being in the war," said Miriam slowly.

"We'll all be in it if it lasts long enough," he replied, with a laugh.

They were both walking very slowly, and seemed absolutely oblivious of the other strollers who were now passing in large numbers in both directions.

"Oh, I'm so disappointed, Montie, that you won't be back at Buckroe Beach this summer. All year I've carried the memory of those two happy weeks last August. I did so want to spend another vacation there this summer. But without you it could never be the same."

"Cheer up, girlie, the worst hasn't happened yet, and if I don't go to camp, I'll probably be right back at the beach, pulling out foolish ladies who walk into deep water."

"And getting equally foolish ladies into deep water who allow you to teach them to swim," she laughed.

Montie squeezed her arm. They lapsed into silence. Both were busy with their thoughts.

Miriam Pinckney was not the first girl that Montgomery Jackson had been interested in. As a matter of fact, each summer for the past three years he had picked up two or three "crushes" at the beach. But when summer was over, his little flirtations became memories. The girls had returned home and he had gone back south to college. For a while the photographs of his latest "loves" would adorn the dresser of his dormitory room, but one by one they would disappear as their space was needed.

"Away, fair lady, into the drawer of forgotten women!" was Roscoe Simms' inevitable remark, whenever his room-mate would add another to the collection in his bottom drawer.

But Miriam's picture had survived. She had looked upon Montie and Roscoe all year now, with those same laughing eyes that had so interested Bob Casper that very morning.

Montie didn't know whether or not he was in love with Miriam. He had only known her for the two weeks that she had spent at the beach the previous summer. As life-guard he had naturally volunteered to teach her to swim. This was the beginning of the friendship that had lasted all year. They had corresponded regularly. They had remembered each other's birthdays, and at Christmas time they had ex-changed gifts. There had never been a girl in his life before who made any difference, and Montie admitted to himself that Miriam did. That was as far as he was able to go.

After the fellows had gone home, and the rest of the folks had retired to their rooms, Miriam opened the French windows that led out to the tiny back porch overlooking the garden in the rear of the house. She pulled out a wicker rocking chair from her room, and sat looking out into the cool, clear night. The air was fragrant with honeysuckle. The noises of the city had long since died away. Miriam was conscious of a sense of complete peace.

Although she had prevented Montie from kissing her that evening when he took leave of her in the parlor down-stairs, she had not resented the attempt. In fact, she was rather proud that he had wanted to kiss her. Miriam had not been attending a co-educational college for two years in vain. The way of men was no closed book to her. The instruction that she had received off the campus, and for which she paid no tuition and received no credit toward graduation, was as valuable to her as her class-room work.

Until she had gone up to Ohio to college, Miriam had been reared in a convent-like school for girls in a very small town in North Carolina. Here she had formed a fast friendship with one of her teachers, a young girl, not much her senior, and fresh from college in New England. In spite of racial differences, the two girls had become inseparable companions.

Miriam's friendship with Frieda Bentley, her teacher, had made an indelible impression on the young southern girl. It had cured her of the awe and fear of white people which she had brought to school with her from her home in South Carolina. Furthermore, she soon learned that all white people were not the ogres and beasts that she had been taught to believe; and finally, it had effectively destroyed the inferiority complex which she had attached to herself and to her own people.

Young Frieda Bentley, who had only a theoretical knowledge of race prejudice herself, was lonely for a companion more nearly her age than the gray-haired, straight-laced spinsters, who comprised the rest of the faculty. Under this natural stimulus, the formal relations of teacher and pupil rapidly ripened into a firm and intimate friendship. Miriam had even gone north during her senior year at the prep school to attend Frieda's wedding. At the Bentley home she had been made as welcome as any of the other guests. The contact that Miriam had with white people as a result of her friendship with Frieda Bentley, developed in this young southern girl a new point of view on the race question.

VI

"Hello, is that you?"

"Who is this, please?"

"You must've been out in the garden eating worms. I've been holding this phone for ten minutes, while they found you."

"But who is it, please?"

"If your ear for music is as bad as your ear for voice, you don't need that job out in the country."

"Oh, I know who it is now! Whatever made you call me up?"

"Wanted to talk to you."

"'Bout what?"

"Lots of things."

"For instance?"

"How to win the war," he chuckled.

They laughed.

"Did your conference turn out o. k.?" she continued.

"Tell you all about it when I see you."

"When you see me!"

"Can't I?"

"I—I hadn't thought about it—it's all such a surprise."

"But I stayed over to-day purposely to see you. I should have gone back last night or early this morning. Come on, be a good sport!"

"Well—just what do you suggest?" replied Miriam, slowly.

"I'm going to dinner with a friend at the officers' mess this evening. I'll be there until about eight o'clock. He has a roadster that he has promised to let me use. If you'll walk out on the right hand side of Vine Street in the direction of the station about eight-fifteen to-night, I'll pass by and pick you up."

"You should make an excellent army officer," was her reply.

"Why?" asked Bob, curiously.

"Because you lay your plans so carefully, even to the tiniest detail."

"Come on! What do you say?"

"That's just it; I really don't know what to say."

"Don't you want to see me?"

"That's a rather pointed question."

"Still, you haven't answered me."

"I confess I don't know what to say."

"Why make a problem out of it?" he asked.

"It is a problem, without my making it one," Miriam replied.

"Well then, let me solve it for you."

"How?"

"By meeting me on Vine Street at eight-fifteen to-night. I must go now, I hear Hendricks coming up the steps. See you later. Bye!"

"Hello, hello," called Miriam, excitedly working the receiver-hook up and down. "Hello, hello!"

"Number please," came the mechanical voice on the other end of the wire.

"I was speaking with a party," stammered Miriam.

"I'm sorry, but your party's hung up," concluded the operator.

Slowly Miriam replaced the receiver, and thoughtfully turned away from the phone.

If Toussaint Pinckney had not died the previous March, his niece Miriam probably would not have been strolling leisurely out Vine Street at eight-fifteen one night in the following June. Miriam's father had died when she was five years old, and Uncle Toussaint had been looking after her ever since. His little tailoring establishment in Columbia had been the means of keeping his brother's child in school. During Miriam's sophomore year in college his health had failed rapidly. After his death, Miriam's financial difficulties almost swamped her, but she managed to stick it out and complete the term. Her mother had been unable to work for years, so Miriam realized that she could not return to college in the Fall. Had she been able to complete her college course, she could have commanded a good position in one of the schools up north. But with only two years college work to her credit, she was restricted to the county schools of the south. Uninteresting, and as poorly paid as this work was, there was no other alternative but domestic service. And Miriam shuddered at the thought. If she could obtain a teaching position in her own county, she would have neither board nor lodging to pay, and her laundry would be done at home, so that practically her entire earnings could be saved toward the completion of her remaining two years in college. Besides, teaching in her own county would keep her near to her mother, who was by no means well.

Ever since she could remember, Miriam had heard of the Caspers, who lived in the big, white house not far from her own home. Although she had never given much thought to the subject, Miriam early acquired the idea that the Caspers represented the leading family in that section of the state. So when fate threw her in the way of Bob Casper, son of the Chairman of the School Board, she considered it a stroke of good fortune. On the other hand, she knew that the situation was fraught with danger. Southern white men, she thought, could only seek friendship with comely colored girls for one purpose—a social equality that existed after dark.

All the afternoon Miriam debated with herself. Should she or should she not go to meet Bob Casper that evening? If there had been any way to reach him by telephone, she would have called him up and told him that she couldn't come. But, of course, she didn't have the slightest idea where to find him. And if she didn't go to meet him, he would be mad as blazes. She remembered that he had stayed over purposely to see her. He must have gone to some trouble, and possibly some expense, to get an automobile for the evening. No, she could never allow him to cruise up and down Vine Street all evening, looking for her. If she angered him that way, he might influence his father to keep her from being appointed. And then he did seem like such a nice fellow, anyway. So interesting, she thought. What a pity! Surely she ought to be able to cope with him. He didn't appear to be the knock-down, drag-out type.

Finally she reached a decision. She would meet him as arranged. But instead of getting in the car with him, she would tell him frankly, but in a nice way, why she couldn't go with him. She would appeal to his reason; convince him without offending him; and leave him thinking what a fine girl she was. Then he would be ready and willing to help her get that job from his father.

Matters didn't work out for Miriam, however, exactly as she had planned. She hadn't gone three blocks from the house when she heard the faint toot of a horn, and Bob Casper was drawing up to the curb near the corner. He was in a small roadster with the top thrown back. Miriam's heart was pounding away. She quickened her step, involuntarily, and started toward the car. At the same moment she recognized the familiar figures of Montie Jason and Roscoe Simms crossing the street diagonally in the middle of the next block, and coming in her direction.

"Quick," she whispered to Bob as she stepped through the open door and sat down beside him, "whisk around this corner, for Heaven's sake."

The motor was still running. Bob stepped on the gas. The car roared around the corner, and was vanishing up the street just as Montie and Roscoe arrived at the crossing.

"Damn, but that girl looked like Miriam!" exclaimed Montie.

"Miriam?" cried Roscoe. "You've got her on your mind! Those were fays* you poor sap."

The chums continued on to Number 39, only to learn from Mrs. Reed that neither of the girls were at home.

"Tell them we'll hunt them up again to-morrow night," said Montie. Dejectedly, they turned their faces back toward the campus.

* white people

VII

"I just thought you'd come," said Bob as the lights of the city disappeared behind them. The car was breezing along the pike and headed for the open country.

Miriam was silent. Bob glanced at her for a split-second.

"What's the matter?" he questioned. "Aren't you enjoying it?"

"Oh yes, the breeze is delightful," she replied, arousing herself now, "but it all happened so suddenly, I haven't fully recovered yet."

"Were you very frightened?"

"Yes, I had an awful scare. Those two fellows that were crossing the street were coming to call on me."

"Do they mean anything to you?"

"Oh, just friends. But I never could have explained it to them. It's all so very unconventional."

"That's what makes it so interesting—so, what shall I say, romantic?"

After that they returned to their silence again. The car sped on. Finally Bob turned off the pike into a narrow, heavily-shaded lane.

"Surely you're not going up into this road?" asked Miriam quickly.

"Oh no," he replied, with a little laugh, "I'm only pulling in here to back out and turn around."

Miriam was glad that it was dark so that he couldn't see the relief on her face.

When the car was turned and headed back to town, Bob pulled over to the side of the road, stopped the motor and switched off the lights.

"Now," he said, "we can chat a bit. I enjoy talking to you."

"I don't feel very talkative to-night, however; I'm afraid you'll find me extremely dull."

"I don't think you could be dull if you wanted to be."

"To be frank with you, Mr. Casper, I really didn't plan to

come out here with you to-night. After the sudden end to our phone conversation this morning, I was in a quandary. I felt that you were expecting me to see you according to your plan, and I didn't want you riding up and down Vine Street all evening, looking for me. So I had kept the appointment only to tell you that I couldn't go driving with you, when I ran into those boys. The only escape that I had was to do just what I did."

"Well, now that you have come, in spite of yourself, are you sorry? You haven't been hurt, have you?"

"Oh, I never thought that you might hurt me. Not you—a Casper!"

"If you feel that way, why didn't you want to come out?"

"Well, it's just not the sort of thing that's done here in the South, to any good purpose," Miriam replied.

"Why the South? Is it done in the North without shattering convention?"

"Prejudice exists in the North, I admit," she answered, "but not nearly so strong. I have attended a co-educational college in Ohio, and I have visited in the homes of white friends in New England. The very best friend that I have is a white girl. Up there, one can occasionally get away from the race problem, and feel like a human being. But down here it's different."

"But I knew several fellows in college," Bob countered, "who used to speak of friends they had among the women of your race."

"Friends?" asked Miriam, bitterly.

"Don't you think it's possible for a man and a woman of different races to have a clean friendship?"

"Of course I do—in some parts of the world—but not here in the South. Laws as well as tradition prohibit that."

"No laws, nor any amount of tradition can prevent two people from falling in love," Bob answered.

"But how far can love go without the protection of law?" Miriam asked.

"You speak about love like an authority," he laughed.

"But I've never been in love in my life," she protested.

"That's interesting."

They laughed together and then dropped into silence.

Miriam finally spoke. "What am I to do when I get back home? Go to see your father?"

"You mean about the school work?"

"Yes, I don't want to delay matters. He might find somebody else."

"Suppose you let me take it up with him first. Then I'll get in touch with you. It may not even be necessary for you to see him."

"But you're so busy with your own plans and what not, I'm afraid you might forget," she said.

"I couldn't be too busy to forget you," he replied softly.

Then breaking the silence that followed his last remark, he asked, "Shall we be going?"

"Just as you say," Miriam replied.

The starter churned. The motor hummed. The glazed road slipped like a ribbon beneath them. Miriam rested her head on the back of the seat and closed her eyes. The breeze cooled her cheeks like a soothing lotion.

"Where shall I let you out?" asked Bob as they neared the starting point.

"Oh, are we home already?" asked Miriam, looking about her.

"Did you enjoy it?" he said.

"Ever so much. I'll get out a couple of blocks this side of Vine Street."

The car slowed down.

"Can I meet you to-morrow night, right here, at the same time, if I can get the roadster?" asked Bob.

"But I thought you were going back home," she said, in surprise.

"Oh, I don't have to. I can wire my folks, you know. I'll get home before I go to camp. But I much prefer being here, if you'll let me see you occasionally."

"Two successive nights—do you call that occasionally?"

He laughed. Miriam liked his laugh. It made him look so boyish. It was an infectious laugh. Whenever he laughed she felt like laughing, too.

"I'll be going to war soon," he said, looking at her and smiling. "Shall I expect you to-morrow night?"

"But suppose you can't get the car?"

"Then I'll call you up," he replied, "but I'm sure it will be o. k."

"All right then, I'll be here," she said.

VIII

"Where in the world have you been keeping yourself?"

Montie was seated on a bench in Mrs. Reed's yard. Miriam had just come out on the porch. It was late in the afternoon, but the day had been exceptionally warm, and the sun still had a lot of spite in it. Montie was fanning himself with his straw hat.

"You look warm, Montie," was Miriam's only reply.

"Burning up. I hurried over here to see if I could catch you before you went out for the evening. I've been here five nights straight without getting a glimpse of you. Didn't you get my messages?"

"Of course, I did; but always after I had made an engagement for the next night. You see, I'm not going to be here very long, and what entertainment I'm going to get must be crowded into a short space. And I've been expecting you to come over during the day, anyhow."

"I can't figure out what you find to do in this town. After school's closed it's the deadest place I've ever been in my life," commented Montie. "Are you busy this evening? Freddie Brown's sister is having a sort of a lawn party out to her aunt's place, and I came over to ask you to go with me. Roscoe has already spoken to Hazel, I believe."

"Yes, Hazel told me about it when I came in last night.

But I had already made an engagement for to-night. I'm awfully sorry."

"Goodness, Miriam, you might give me one evening," he protested. "I'll be going in a day or two now."

"Any news of the camp?"

"That's just it. The camp opens in a few days at Ft. Des Moines, Iowa, and I am going to take the exam to-morrow. That's why I've been so anxious to see you. Can't you possibly get out of your engagement to-night?"

"I—I really—I don't see how I can," she replied very slowly.

"Don't I mean anything to you any more, Miriam?" Montie asked softly.

Miriam laid her hand on his arm. "Don't be foolish, silly boy," she said laughing, "I'm going to miss you a lot when you go to camp."

"Miss me! When I go? You haven't seen anything of me since you've been here!"

"But there is a certain amount of comfort in just knowing that you are around, Montie," said Miriam.

"Comfort! Who wants to be a comfort to anybody!"

"I'm sorry if I hurt you, you know I didn't mean to," she replied quickly.

Montie stood up. "Well, it's too bad you're dated up for to-night," he said with a shrug of the shoulders. "I must be getting on now. Roscoe is waiting for me. We're going out to the Brown's place with Dr. Bush; he has a new touring car. Sorry you won't be along."

"So am I. Come by and tell me all about the exam to-morrow morning. I'll be expecting you."

"What's she hitting now, Doc?"

Dr. Bush glanced admiringly at his speedometer.

"Oh, about forty," he replied.

"Forty!" exclaimed his wife from the back seat. "Charlie, that service man told you not to drive this car over twenty-five miles an hour for the next two weeks. You're going to break something, sure."

"You leave that to me, sister," called back the proud doctor over his shoulder, as the car glided along through the night.

The rotund Roscoe was wedged in between Mrs. Bush and Hazel on the back seat. "Let 'im alone, it's his party," he chuckled.

Montie, who was riding up front with Dr. Bush, turned and spoke to Hazel. "Are you enjoying it, Hazel?"

"It's wonderful. I never saw the moon so full," she replied. "I don't care if we never get there."

"We're nearly there now," said the doctor, "it's not over five or six more miles."

Suddenly the car began to lag. In spite of Dr. Bush's efforts to give it more gas, it was evident that the motor was going to stop.

"I'm not getting any gas," he said, puzzled.

"Are you out of gas, do you think?" asked Montie.

· "Don't see how I could be; I just put in fifteen gallons about an hour ago."

"I told you, Charlie, that you were driving this car too fast. One of these days you'll listen to something that I say," complained his wife.

"Don't start that I-told-you-so stuff out here, for pity sake. I'll have it running again in a few minutes." The doctor guided the car to the edge of the road. The motor stopped. He and Montie climbed out and took off their coats.

After several minutes investigation under the hood, the doctor finally ventured a diagnosis.

"When a motor stops like this it's due to either one of two things; it's not getting any gas, or it's not getting a spark. It's not the gas, because the carburetor is flooded now, and the tank is nearly full. There's something wrong with the juice. Probably a wire has become loosened and jumped its connection. It's easy to fix if we can find the wire. We need a flash-light, though. Just my luck not to have one, either."

"You couldn't try a match, could you?" asked Montie.

"Not now," replied Bush, "gas is still running out of the carburetor, and it's all over everything."

"I'll stand out in the road and see if I can get somebody to stop. We may pick up a flash-light," volunteered Montie.

"We haven't passed two cars since we left town," said Roscoe from the back seat.

"There's a car parked around that bend a couple of hundred yards ahead," said Dr. Bush, "I just caught a glimpse of its tail-light through the trees."

"Good, I'll walk on down there, and see if I can borrow a light," Montie suggested.

"If they haven't a flash, maybe they'll turn around and throw their head-lights on my motor until I locate the trouble."

"You stay here and help Doc, Montie, I'll go," said Roscoe, as he laboriously extricated himself from the depths of the back seat.

Alone, Roscoe set off at a leisurely pace down the road. As he neared the parked car in front of him, he debated with himself whether or not he should approach quietly from behind, or run the risk of scaring them off by letting them know that he was coming. He was on the verge of whistling.

"Guess I better play safe," he cautioned himself, "they may think I'm a hold-up man or a cop, and speed away before I can get near enough to them to tell them what I want."

Accordingly, he took to the side of the road and approached the car under the shadow of the trees along the edge. Once around the bend he came upon the car suddenly. The top was back and he could clearly see a man sitting in the driver's seat. Otherwise, the car looked empty.

"I beg your pardon," said Roscoe loudly, emerging from the shadow, and crossing behind the car to the driver's seat, "but we're stuck on the road about three hundred yards back and—Miriam! What in the world are you doing out here!"

The silence was tense. Roscoe transferred his gaze from Miriam to Bob Casper. Not a soul moved. Nobody dared to breathe. The air seemed charged. Then in a quiet tone Roscoe said simply, "Miriam, I didn't know you were such a fool."

He turned and walked back in the direction he had come. The moon continued to shine. Somewhere a dog barked. Then a motor started, hummed and the sound died away in the distance.

"You didn't stay long, Roscoe," the doctor greeted him as he came up. "Any luck?"

"Not a bit!" was the laconic reply.

"What'd they say about coming down and giving us a little light?"

"Wouldn't do that either," he replied.

"I heard them drive off a few minutes ago. Must've been a bunch o' crackers," the doctor added. "Well, we'll just have to do the best we can, and feel for the wires with a little help from the moon," he philosophized.

Montie and Bush, bent over the motor, worked together. Roscoe paced silently up and down the road. The women gossiped quietly on the back seat.

"Well I'm a son-of-a-gun!" exclaimed the doctor several minutes later. "Here's the darned trouble right in front of our eyes. The center wire has jumped out of the distributor. Come on fellows, hop in! Everything's pretty now. My hands are a mess, though."

IX

"Well, that's that!" cried Montie as he burst into his room about noon of the day following the Brown's party.

"Did they say you could be a Major-general?" asked Roscoe, quietly.

"Damn, but you're lazy," commented Montie, eyeing his room-mate stretched at full length across the bed, with his hands clasped under his head. "You were in the same spot when I left here three hours ago."

Roscoe let the remark pass.

"What's the matter with you, fella?" continued Montie. "You've been in the dumps since last night. Didn't you have a good time at the party?"

"How'd you make out with the camp examination?" asked Roscoe ignoring his chum's question.

"I know that I'm physically fit," said Montie slowly, "but the captain remarked that I was awfully young."

"Did many take it?" Roscoe inquired.

"The place was crowded. They came from all over the State. Come on, walk over to Vine Street with me. I promised to hunt up Miriam after the exam was over."

"Hell, it's too hot to go out now," pleaded Roscoe.

"Don't be so lazy," replied Montie.

"But suppose they're out," Roscoe protested.

"She's expecting me," said Montie, confidently.

Roscoe sat up in the bed with a start. He parted his lips to speak. Slowly they closed again as he sat there staring at Miriam's photo on the dresser.

"What the hell's the matter with you, Roscoe?" cried Montie, impatiently. "You act like a cokie."

Roscoe smiled. It was a wan sickly effort. "Let's go, if you insist," he said, reaching for his hat.

Montie looked at him sharply, but said nothing. The two of them left the room together, silently.

When they reached the colored section of town, their attention was attracted to a small, uninviting-looking store, which lay on their way. In Negro parlance the place was known as a "pig-foot joint." In front of the shop a small dilapidated black-board served as a menu card. The board, in a badly scrawled hand, announced a bill of fare of "chittlins, hog-maws, pig-nuckles, sanwitches of all kinds and soft drinks." Painted in large white letters with a blue edge, across the front of the window, was the caption, "Mary Dew's Cafe." The show window was empty except for two large placards: one was the announcement of a dance, and the other bore the inscription "Hot rolls Sunday mornings." The back of the window was decorated with a torn lace curtains that was yellowing with age and dust. But the most prominent feature of the place, both inside and out, was the flies.

Montie and Roscoe noticed two white soldiers inside the store. One of them was smoking a newly lighted cigar and the other held a bottle of "pop" in his hand. Two gaudily dressed Negro girls were leaning over the little counter, talking with the soldiers. Peals of loud, coarse laughter found their way into the street, continually.

"That's the kind of thing I hate," remarked Montie as they passed the front of the store.

"There's a lot of that going on around here now, with all these soldiers in town," commented Roscoe, without taking his eye off the side-walk in front of him.

"Women like that haven't got a damn bit of self-respect," continued Montie, looking back.

"Hell, you don't look for self-respect among that type, do you?" replied Roscoe, still gazing fixedly ahead.

The two went back to their silence and trudged on. When they reached the Reed's gate, Roscoe stepped back and let Montie go through first.

"Hello, Hazel, is Miriam in?" asked Montie.

"Hello, there," replied Hazel, "why, Miriam went home this morning."

"Home?" repeated Montie, almost breathlessly. "This morning? Why she's only been here a week. I thought she was to stay a week longer. Is there anything wrong at home?"

"Not that I know of," continued Hazel. "Miriam was awake when I got in last night from the party. She came into my room and told me that she was leaving in the morning for home. I tried to argue with her, but she wouldn't let me talk. Her mind was made up, she said. I never saw her so nervous and excited before. Something's wrong. But for the life of me, I can't figure it out. She left at eight o'clock this morning."

"Well I'll bless my soul!" exclaimed Montie. "Yep! You're right, Hazel. Something's come over Miriam. Maybe I got on her nerves. Well, if you write her tell her I kept my engagement with her."

"Do you want her address?" enquired Hazel.

"I have it; but I'm not going to write her. Not until I hear from her," replied Montie, with decisiveness.

"Cheer up, Montie," said Roscoe, laying his hand affectionately on his friend's shoulder. "Wait till you come back from the wars a Major-general, you'll have all the girls you can use."

As the two pals turned into the campus on their return trip, Roscoe suddenly stopped and faced his friend. "Say Montie, were you very much in love with Miriam?"

"I didn't know it until now," replied Montie, without hesitation.

X

"I hear we're pulling out for the big city by the end of the week, Sarge."

"Damn! whar'd yo' get that frum, boy?" asked the sergeant, enthusiastically.

"Grape-vine telegraph." Private Montgomery Jason hastened across the company street to deliver a message to the Major, leaving the excited sergeant to spread the good news.

And how the news did spread! New York's National Guard regiment of colored soldiers had been in camp on the outskirts of Spartanburg nearly all summer. There had been numerous petty clashes with the townspeople and soldiers from other units quartered in the vicinity. The air

of Spartanburg was different from that of Harlem. Men
and officers alike were happy at the thought of going back
north.

When Montgomery Jason found that his name was not
included in the quota that went from his state to the Officers Training Camp at Ft. Des Moines, he was bitterly
disappointed. In spite of his youth, he felt that he would
make a much better officer than a good many of the older
men who had been selected. Montie knew that what he
lacked in years, he more than made up for in enthusiasm.
His mother had been his only comfort during the ensu-
ing days of worry and uncertainty. He had lingered around
Sumpter for nearly three weeks, although his old job at
Buckroe Beach was still waiting for him. But the beach
might have meant Miriam, and she was the very last per-
son in the world he wanted to see—or even think about.
He had neither seen nor heard of her since she left Spartanburg. He concluded bitterly that she had quit him cold.

Then came the news that the New York regiment had
arrived in Spartanburg for training.

"I'll go up and see if I can enlist," he told his mother, enthusiastically. "Maybe I can work my way up through the
ranks and get a commission, after all. It's better than being
drafted and probably put in a labor battalion."

The Colonel had been so impressed with Montie's ap-
pearance and his enthusiasm, that in spite of the fact that
the regiment had been virtually recruited up to full strength
before it left New York, Montie was assigned to Company
"L" of the 3rd Battalion. He was a bit disappointed to learn
that all of the colored officers had either been left behind
or had been transferred to other outfits. But this did not
dampen his determination to earn a commission.

Promotions were slow, however. September found him
still in the ranks—still a buck private. Very few changes
were made in the non-commissioned personnel. But now
he was delighted with the prospects of a trip to New York.
He burned with excitement as he burst into the Major's

tent with orders for the Battalion commander to report to Regimental Headquarters immediately.

During his tour of guard duty that day, Montie had been assigned as orderly in the Colonel's headquarters. With eyes and ears wide open he had made two important discoveries. One, he had already put into circulation, that the outfit had been ordered back to New York. The other was that because the regiment had now been "federalized," there was going to be a general shake-up of the officers. Several of the older officers were to be promoted and transferred to other regiments, and a new batch of officers, mostly second-lieutenants fresh from the training camps, were being sent on in their places.

"It's a darn shame that they don't give some of us fellows a chance," he remarked to himself on his way back to quarters that night. "I'll bet we'll pick up a bunch of crackers, too, from around these parts."

"Come in Lieutenant. What can I do for you, this morning?"

"Good morning, Captain Mitchell, I have a favor to ask of you."

"A favor? It will be a pleasure, I'm sure," replied the good-natured Captain.

"First of all let me get my bearings correct. Have you a private in this Company by the name of Jason? Montgomery Jason is the full name," said the Lieutenant, consulting a letter which he held open before him.

"Tell you in a minute, I'll call the Company clerk. Corporal French!" shouted the Captain.

A short, chubby, very black soldier with a pencil behind his ear, entered through an open door and stood at attention. "Yes sir!" he said.

"Corporal, have we a Private Jason in this outfit?" asked the Company Commander.

"Yes sir. Third platoon, Lieutenant Mahoney, sir!" responded the clerk, readily.

"That's all, Corporal."

"Thanks, Cap," continued the Lieutenant, "this is purely a personal matter, but I have a big interest in that boy. He's from my part of the country, and he's pretty well educated. I think he'd make a darn good non-com. Anything that you can do for him along that line, I will consider as a direct favor to me."

"I'll make a note of it, Casper, and when Mahoney comes in I'll speak to him, too. From the news that came down this morning, we'll be having lots of vacancies, and lots of promotions pretty soon."

"You don't say! Are we going up?" asked Lieutenant Robert Lee Casper, in evident delight.

"Yep! We're to be brigaded with the French and shoved right in."

"Well, between you and me, Cap, I'm damn glad. I'm sick of this training area stuff, first in the States and then over here for the last three months. I've been in the army now for damn near ten months, and all I know about the war is what I read about it. I'm fed up."

"Don't worry, you'll get yours. From now on it's going to be different. Our fellows have been catchin' hell up front. By the way, I hear you have a new Battalion Commander over there. What's his name?"

"Davis," replied Bob Casper, "seems to be a fine fellow, too. I like your Major though, used to be in the regular army, I believe, wasn't he?"

"Yes, some time ago—served a couple of enlistments, I heard."

"Well Cap, I'll be seeing you again. Thanks for the Jason matter. If I can ever repay the favor, call on me. I'm over in the 2nd Battalion, 'H' Company, you know. Good luck."

XI

It was pouring rain. It had been raining all day. From the looks of things it probably was going to rain all night. The 3rd Battalion was soaked to the skin. Packs were double their normal weight due to the water that they had absorbed.

The Battalion had been hiking in the rain ever since they left their trucks at noon. And now night was almost on them. All afternoon they had been passing through one deserted, shell-shattered village after another. In the distance they could hear a constant rumble that reminded them of thunder. As darkness settled upon them, the thunder grew louder and louder and was accompanied by sudden flashes of light that illuminated the rain-drenched countryside.

The men trudged along silently under their burdens. The relentless rain continued to beat down. The incessant rumble grew closer and closer. The tramp of hob-nailed feet gave out a dead, hollow sound. Although the soldiers were physically exhausted, the uncertainty of their whereabouts, and a growing sense of danger, gave strength to their tiring limbs.

Finally after an unusually long halt, the order came to fall-in in two columns of files, one on each side of the road. The officers walked near the middle of the roadway. The going was very slow now. The road was full of shell holes and covered with debris in many places.

Montie found himself plodding along by Lieutenant Mahoney.

"Hell, we can't go much farther," said the Lieutenant, "the head of this column must be pretty nearly up to the front by now."

"Are we going in to-night, Lieutenant?" asked Montie in a hoarse whisper.

"Who knows," answered Mahoney, "nobody ever tells you anything in the army."

They were now approaching the outskirts of another of the demolished villages. The road, of course, led through the center of the town. Unroofed houses with their stark walls silhouetted against the gray sky stood out like tombstones in a country church-yard.

Suddenly there was a terrific roar. It seemed almost in front of them. Then came a screeching, whistling, sickening noise. It grew louder and louder. "Down!" somebody screamed.

Montie made a headlong dive for the ditch by the road. He struck the ground. There was a thunderous explosion. He was conscious of a deafening, metallic sound in his ears. He thought that he had been hit. He was waiting to die.

"God, I thought I'd swallowed that one," said the Lieutenant in the ditch beside him, "but it was only our tin helmets in collision."

"I thought I was dead," breathed Montie. It was his first shell.

"Here comes another!" cried the Lieutenant.

They huddled there together, the black man and the white, each seeking the protection of the others body. Fifteen minutes later, when the shelling had subsided they climbed out, and the column moved on.

"They have the range of this road, and they know that it's used at night, so I guess we can expect this at regular intervals," remarked Mahoney, as he moved along the line to check up on any losses.

At the next halt, half way up the slope of a thickly-wooded hill, the order was passed along the column, "Fall out in these woods, and make yourselves comfortable for the night. No lights!"

Morning brought some relief from the rain but none from the dampness. The thick woods were soaking wet. The sky was still gray and overcast. The slope was teeming with soldiers. Two battalions of the regiment were concealed in the thicket. Everything was deathly quiet. The Major in command of the 3rd Battalion was holding a council of war with his officers in a ravine near the foot of the slope.

"From all sources—intelligence service, prisoners and from aerial observations, the Boche are planning a general attack along this front in order to straighten out their lines on both sides of the river," the Major said. "This battalion occupies a position on the extreme right, in reserve. Our right flank rests on the river, which is just over that knoll. Our lines on this side of the river are about a quarter of a mile in advance of our positions on the other side. We can't expect any help from that side of the river; but, on the other hand, we will be subject to a cross fire from the machine guns of the Boche who are now directly across on our flank."

The Major paused and asked the Adjutant for a map. After studying the map for a moment, he resumed, "If the French up in front of us are beaten back, which is very probable, we are to move up and occupy that line of support trenches at the top of this hill. And we've got to stick, gentlemen. This battalion is to stay in those trenches until the last man is flicked out. If the French decide to counter-attack they will re-form their outfits right here on this slope under our protection, and we will go over with them. Companies 'I' and 'L' will occupy the left and right flanks of the battalion front, respectively. Companies 'K' and 'M' will form the center. Messages will reach me in that gully up ahead. We believe that the attack will probably start to-morrow morning. The battalion will stand-to at dusk to-night, however, and again at day-break to-morrow, of course. Any questions?"

Late in the afternoon the sun returned to duty. At the evening stand-to the only sign of the enemy was a squadron of Boche planes that passed high overhead, just before dark. During the early part of the night there was an in-

termittent shelling of the road, along which the battalion
had come.

Montie was beginning to get used to the shells now.
The whole battalion, in fact, was becoming more composed
as the shells passed over them and dropped, harmlessly,
in the fields or in the shattered town behind them. The
platoon commanders moved among the men issuing orders in a quiet tone. The soldiers were ready. They had
their orders. Their rifles were in shape—bores clean, bolt
mechanism oiled, cartridges clipped, bayonets gleaming.
The long night finally drew to a close. Dawn was on the
horizon.

"God, anything is better than this waiting," said Montie
to the man next to him as they turned out for stand-to.

"Won't be long now," replied the soldier, laconically.

Before his words had died out there was a sudden, terrific blast. To Montie it seemed like all hell had broken
loose. He knew that the barrage had come. The infantry
attack would soon follow. The deafening, maddening roar
went on. The ground behind them seemed to be boiling,
seething. Fountains of black smoke and pieces of earth
geysered into the air. The stricken town in their rear was
being torn to shreds. Explosions blew away the remnants
of buildings, carried off joists and rafters, smashed walls
and crushed entire dwellings. Everywhere the air was lit-
tered with plaster, timber and stone. White dust and smoke
mingled in a medley. The shell-bursts lost their individu-
ality and combined into one massive and uninterrupted
symphony. The battalion, protected by the slope of the hill,
gazed awe-stricken at the volcano before their eyes. The
whole world was in eruption.

Like the subsiding of a torrential rain, the barrage died
out as suddenly as it commenced. Then came a sound new
to the ears of the hidden troops—the riveting of a thousand machine guns. From across the river the Germans
showered a hail of lead into the French trenches. The

French, seeking to stem the tide of the advancing gray hordes, rushed to their own machine gun emplacements that had survived the artillery barrage, and swept the open plain, as the Boche pressed forward. The men of Montie's battalion, huddled against the side of the wooded hill heard the relentless rat-tat-tat of the chorus of machine guns and the sickly whine of the steady stream of bullets that passed over the crest of the hill.

Early in the fore-noon came a runner from Battalion Headquarters. The French were dropping back. The 3rd Battalion was ordered up. In a thin line of skirmishers the companies moved up the hill. As they neared the crest the hell became intensified. A deadly flow of lead was sweeping the support trenches from the machine gun batteries across the river. The soldiers lay flat on the ground. They advanced by inches, seeking imaginary shelter behind each twig or stump. The death spray never relaxed. The incessant tapping of the riveting machine guns was interspersed only with the anguished groans of the dying, and the cries and curses of the wounded. And yet the line moved forward. A burst of bullets carried off a leg. A sudden hail of lead punctured a chest. A single bullet hurried on its way through a jaw and out by way of the temple. A heart was shattered. But the line pushed on.

Montie Jason reached the support trenches in company with the surviving members of his squad. They literally fell into the earth. They had become automatons. Reason had long since left them. Death, at the hands of an invisible foe, stalked them on every side. They dared not lift a head above the parapet. The leaden hail was sweeping close to the ground.

Suddenly they were frightened by a roar directly behind them. With a sickening of the heart, Montie heard the screeching of shells once more. But this time the shells were traveling in the opposite direction. They were falling on the other side of the river among the German machine gun nests. It was a battery of seventy-fives, someone said. The effect was instantaneous. The riveting died down under the shelling of the battery, and the handful of harrassed French in the front lines fell back in good order to the support trenches, now that the machine guns on their flank had been silenced.

"Heah dey comes!" screamed a sergeant. "Let 'em have it!"

Montie saw a line of gray forms moving carefully through the broken wire and abandoned trenches down the slope in front of him. A French machine gun at his right barked into action just at that moment. Automatically, he pulled the trigger of his rifle. A gray form slumped on the wire. Again and again he pulled. The man on his left groaned.

"God, I'm hit," he cried. "The bastards!"

Like the dash of surf against a rocky shore, the gray waves were hurled back each time they tried to mount the slope.

Just before dusk Lieutenant Mahoney came into the trench where Montie and the remnants of his squad were carrying on.

"Where's Corporal Galloway?" he asked, nervously.

"Got hit befo' we ever got into dis trench," spoke up the nearest man.

"The Captain's been hit, too," replied Lieutenant Mahoney, wearily, as he ran his eye along the men on the fire-step. "Jason, take charge of this squad," he continued. "After a short artillery preparation we're going to counter-attack. As soon as the barrage lifts the whole battalion will fight its way forward to those trenches that the French abandoned this morning. When we get there we've got to hang on, do you hear. During the night we'll dig in a little better and repair the wire. Don't go over until you hear my whistle. The artillery will open up just about dark. You men might relax for a few minutes now. Things are quieting down."

The Lieutenant disappeared as suddenly as he came.

"Well, Bo, you's a Corpril now!" said one of Montie's squad-mates, poking him playfully in the ribs.

"But for how long?" answered Montie, squatting on the fire-step. "Think we'll ever reach those trenches, Jackson?"

"Damn right we will—some of us will, anyhow! I'd give a mont's pay for a col' bottle o' beer, right now," replied the soldier, pushing his helmet back off his head, and wiping his forehead with his coat sleeve.

Montie smiled, but said nothing.

"There's the whistle! Let's go, gang!" cried Montie, climbing out of the trench.

All along the front black men were scrambling out of trenches—ducking, jumping, running, sometimes crawling—but always forward. The 75's were thundering across the river, driving the Boche machine gunners to cover. The Germans, up ahead in their newly gained trenches strove vainly to halt the black advance. One by one, however, the maxims were silenced by hand grenade and cold steel. Wave after wave swept forward. There were always two to take the place of one that had fallen.

"This is far enough," cried Montie, panting, as he jumped into a trench beside the last three members of his squad. "Was Jackson badly hit? I saw him go down, poor devil."

"Machine gun got 'im in the stomach," replied one of the others. "It was hell, wasn't it?"

XII

Laval, judged by American standards, was undoubtedly a "hick" town. But after ten days on the front, it was a Garden of Eden to Montie Jason. Small as Laval was, it accommodated the remnants of two companies of the 3rd Battalion, "L" and "M." About three kilometers down the road, Villaines, a larger town, sheltered Regimental Head-quarters and one company from the 2nd Battalion.

Montie was now Sergeant Jason, of the 3rd Platoon of Company "L."

"How long we goin' stay heah, Sarge?" inquired a cor-poral, as Montie sauntered down the village street.

"You're not in a hurry to leave, are you?" laughed Montie.

"Hell, no!" replied the other.

"Nobody knows," said Sergeant Jason, "but we've got to get some replacements before we can go back up yonder."

"Ah ain' exackly in no hurry to git back up there," con-cluded the corporal, as he turned into the estaminet.

As Montie passed Company Headquarters, he was hailed by Lieutenant Thatcher, who was now in command of the company.

"Sergeant, we're getting in some replacements from the Depot Brigade tomorrow, and we've got to make room for them."

"Yes, sir," replied Montie.

"I want you and three other non-coms to move out of your billets with the men. Do you see that last house down the road, on the other side of the street—the house with the wall around it—well, there're two rooms down there, according to this billeting list. We have plenty of accom-modations for our officers, so you non-coms move down there to-day. It's a little out of the way, but we need the space. That'll give some room in the billets for the replace-ments. I'm afraid the men will have to double up, anyhow."

"Thank you, Lieutenant. It will be a treat to sleep in a bed." Montie saluted, and hurried off to find three other sergeants, and to roll his pack.

"I'm ready so I'll go on ahead," Montie was saying a few minutes later. The other sergeant was down on his knees, assembling the contents of his pack.

"Yea, you go ahaid, Jason, I'll wait and come 'long with Harris and Campbell. You got to do the talkin' for us any-how," he replied.

When Montie reached the door of the house that Lieutenant Thatcher had pointed out to him, he wished that he had waited for the other sergeants. There was an air of refinement and culture about the place. Its location beyond the edge of town smacked of aloofness. The high garden wall that enclosed it, clothed it with exclusiveness.

"I guess it's too far from the town for the officers," thought Montie, rapping on the door.

He hoped that nobody was home. He felt like an intruder—an uninvited guest. Suppose these people objected. He couldn't force himself on folks of this kind. One could see that they weren't ordinary peasants. Of course, he could always go back to sleeping in the hay-loft. But this was the army, and orders were orders. Still—

Just at that moment a bolt was pulled on the inside and the heavy door swung slowly open.

"Bon jour, Madame," he managed to get off, in his best A. E. F. French.

"Bon jour," sounded off the very be-wrinkled old woman who stood in the open door. Montie felt that he was undergoing a rigid inspection. "Que voulez vous, Monsieur?" she rattled away.

"Une chambre a coucher," replied Montie, very hesitantly.

"Non, non, officier," cried the old woman, making ready to close the door.

"Sous-officier," was the only thing that Montie could think of.

"Non, non, officier," screamed the old woman again, shaking her head vigorously.

"Who is that at the door, grand-mother?" called a voice from within, in French.

"Un noir," called back the old woman, then by way of further explanation, she added, "un Americain."

Montie smiled to himself. "The world over," he thought. "A nigger first—an American afterwards."

There was a movement in the hall behind the old woman.

And then Montie wanted to rub his eyes. There stood the best looking girl that he had seen since he had been in France. He noticed at once that unlike most of the other women, she was not in mourning.

"Bon jour," she greeted him pleasantly, as she came up to the door beside her grand-mother.

"Bon jour, Mademoiselle," he guessed, gaining a little confidence from her pleasing manner.

"Vous parlez francais?" she questioned, with an engaging smile.

"Pas beaucoup—un petit peu," he replied, somewhat abashed.

Both women showed unusual surprise—and interest.

"You speak very well?" said the young woman, in French.

Montie ignored the compliment. "I, and three others, all non-commissioned officers, have been assigned to two rooms here," Montie said with some hesitation.

At this point the two women broke into a rapid-fire discussion—or argument—that reminded Montie somewhat of his machine gun experiences of the past few days. Most of the conversation was lost on him, absolutely. Finally, the younger woman turned to him again and said very slowly, so that he could understand, "We had been told by the French billeting officer who listed our rooms that they would be occupied occasionally by officers. They promised that no enlisted men would be quartered with us, because my grand-mother and I are here alone—and we don't have the usual accommodations for the men, anyhow. But since you have been sent to us we will take care of you and your comrades. C'est la guerre."

When Montie came back to his room that night it had been dark for several hours. After supper he had gone over to Villaines for a stroll, just to see what the town was like, he told himself. When he got back to Laval, where his own company was quartered it was good and dark, so he decided to take a plunge in the canal. Even after he had refreshed himself by his swim, Montie decided that it was too early to go back to his room. He denied to himself that he was purposely waiting to return late so that all of the inmates might be asleep. Yet he couldn't get around the fact that he was tired and sleepy, and the call of that big, feather four-poster was hard to resist. He felt that the other sergeants were probably asleep by now, but somehow he couldn't bring himself to go back until he was reasonably sure that everybody else was in bed. He chided himself for being an intruder. Even worse than that, he felt guilty and responsible for having brought the others here. He wished that he could be as callous and indifferent about such matters as Campbell and the other non-coms. The people had told him definitely that their house was reserved for officers—white men—and here he was, not only intruding himself, but bringing three others with him.

The door was ajar. He tipped in. Montie knew that it had been purposely left open for him. He closed it quietly, bolted it, and gently mounted the stairs to his room. He peeped in on Harris and Campbell to re-assure himself that he had not locked them out. Then he went to his own room. What a relief to get in and close the door behind him! "I bet I'll be out of here before reveille to-morrow morning," was his last thought, as he climbed in beside his room-mate.

For the next three nights Montie came in after everybody else in the house had gone to bed. For the next three mornings he had been the first one out. He had never returned home during the day.

The came disaster to Montie's plans. The Major came over from Battalion Headquarters to inspect companies "L" and "M," and Sergeant Jason had to return to his room early in the fore-noon to get his equipment for the inspection. When he entered the hall-way the sound of a piano in an adjoining room greeted his ears. Like a flash it carried him back to Buckroe Beach and Miriam. He closed the door gently and started for the stair-way. The music stopped, and the young woman whom he had seen the first day came to the door leading into the hall.

"Bon jour," she greeted him with a smile. "Where have you been hiding for the last three days?"

"Not hiding," Montie replied, "just working hard."

"So late at night, and so early in the morning?" she questioned, with a great deal of doubt in her voice.

"C'est la guerre," he answered, moving towards the stairs.

"Because you speak French so well, I wanted you to help me with my English," she ventured, holding aloft an English grammar.

"Oh, are you studying English?" answered Montie in surprise.

"A leetle bit," she replied with a laugh. "Won't you help me?" she continued, going back to the French.

"Yes, I'll be glad to—sometime."

"To-night?" she asked, enthusiastically.

"Oh, not to-night," he replied hastily.

"You may be gone to-morrow. Come home after your supper. It's nice and cool in the garden. Please do," the girl pleaded.

A bugle sounded.

"I must be dashing," Montie answered hurriedly. "All right I'll come over this evening and give you a lesson."

"Have you been to Paris?"

"No, but I hope to, before I go back," Montie answered.

"One hasn't seen France, until he goes to Paris," she said.

The English lesson was over. They were still out in the garden, but it was too dark to read. They were both seated on a wrought-iron bench, in front of a tiny fountain that formed the central motif for the garden.

Montie Jason was the first Negro, as well as the first American, that Blanche Aubertin had ever spoken to in her life. Now that he had lost some of his reticence, there were certain questions that she was just burning to ask him. Montie had a great deal of difficulty in making her understand that South Carolina was just as much a part of the continental United States, as Normandy was a part of France. Then she wanted to know why he was light brown in color, and had soft, wavy, black hair, while the other sergeants were all black, with funny, crinkly hair. Montie was amused at this; but he realized that the amusement was not due to the question itself, but to his own inability to answer it. She was so naive. Then she wanted to know why all the officers were white men. She frowned when she asked this question. Montie sensed that something was wrong. Once again he became wary and timid. He made light of the question and tried to pass on to something else. But she continued, still frowning.

"One of the white officers stopped me on the street in Villaines yesterday, and asked me what my name was and where I lived."

"He just wanted to be friendly," said Montie, reassuringly. "What did you tell him?"

Her eyes snapped and she became very indignant. "I let him know what I didn't live in Villaines, that I lived in Laval. Then I brushed by him and went into a shop. He called me 'keed'," she said, using the English.

Montie tried to laugh it off. "He didn't mean anything. Most of our officers are fine fellows. He probably had one drink too many, and was in a merry mood. Tell me," he continued, in an effort to change the subject, "how is it that you are here alone with your grand-mother?"

"My father is in Paris with the Intelligence Service," she replied, rousing herself out of her former mood, "my mother died when I was a little girl. I go to Paris occasionally to see my father. He comes home on leave once or twice a year. It's very lonely here without him."

Sergeant Jason did not report for duty quite so early the next morning.

XIII

Lieutenant Casper had just started a letter to his father. He hadn't gone very far. As a matter of fact, he had simply written:

"Dear Dad,

Our outfit has been resting in billets for about ten days now. We were terribly cut up in our first engagement. My company lost three officers, and I have just been made a 1st Lieutenant and placed second in command of the company."

Then came an imperative knocking on the door and a voice calling, "Casper! Casper!"

"Hello, Warner, what's up?" asked Bob, slightly annoyed, as the door opened.

"Come on for a ride, there's an old headquarters Dodge downstairs, and Bettis says I might use it for a l'il while," gushed Lieutenant Warner, partly supporting himself against the high poster bed.

"But you can't drive, Charlie, you can hardly stand up," protested Bob.

"Hell, what's matter I can't drive?" asked his friend, indignantly.

"You've been drinking, that's what," replied Bob.

"You mean I'm too drunk to drive? Awright, I'll go by myself. Good evenin'." Warner staggered out of the room, and down the stairs.

"Damn, I ought not let him go off by himself like that," muttered Bob reproachfully, as the car door slammed, "he'll break his neck, sure." He jumped from the table and ran to the window. "Charlie, Charlie!" he called to Warner in the car below the window, "wait for me, I'm coming!"

"Hurry 'long then," cried his friend, "can't keep the pretty gals waitin'."

After a great deal of persuasion, Warner finally agreed to let Bob do the driving.

"Where do you want to go, Charlie?" Bob asked.

"To Laval," answered his companion, immediately.

"Laval? Where the hell is Laval?" asked Bob in surprise.

"How the hell do I know? You said you wanted to drive. Now go to Laval, or by God, I'll drive," declared Warner. "There's a damn Frenchman. Ask him!"

They reached their destination a few minutes later.

"Now where—or what?" queried Bob, amused at his friend. "What in the hell did you want to come to this little dump for?"

Warner sat up in the car and looked around. "See that old French woman over there, drive over to her. Ask her where the prettiest mamaselle in this town lives. Tell 'er she's a blonde, with big blue eyes—and wears a pretty, pink dress."

"Charlie Warner you are the original damn fool!" laughed Bob, proceeding, however, to do as his friend directed.

After prolonged pointing and gesticulating, Bob turned to Warner. "She says there's only one girl here who answers the description you gave. She seems to be doubtful that we're looking for her. Aubertin is her name. She must be the village high-brow. Anyhow, she lives in that big house we just passed. Let's hurry, 'cause it's getting late, and I've got a couple of letters to get off."

"Hello, there's Thatcher over on those steps. Bet he's got a slim li'l drink for me. Wait here. Be right back," cried Warner, getting out of the car and making his way across the street.

"For God's sake, Charlie, get back in the car," called Casper just loud enough to make Warner hear him. But it was no use. He kept going. Bob waited for his friend several minutes, with growing impatience. Just as he was about to go in after him, Lieutenant Thatcher came out to the car.

"Good evening, Lieutenant, I suppose that you are with Warner."

"Yes," replied Bob. "I am."

"Well, he's in a helluva drunk in there on my bed, and I think it's best to let him stay there and sleep it off. If you were to come across the Major or the Colonel with him in that car, it might cost both of you an awful lot of trouble."

"Thanks, Lieutenant; but how'll he get back to Villaines?"

"Oh, that's all right, we'll send him over on a truck or in an ambulance in the morning," laughed Thatcher, as Bob pulled away.

When Bob approached the big house on the road back to Villaines, he chuckled to himself. He had a plan. "Here's where I put a fast one over on Warner." He stopped the car in front of the house. He was shaking with laughter as he walked up the steps. "What a lark!" he thought. Then he caught the sound of music—a piano.

"Doesn't sound much like the war around here," he remarked to himself as he knocked on the door. Above the tones of the piano he could hear an occasional laugh, and the sound of voices.

"They evidently don't hear me," he said to himself, "sounds like a party." He knocked again.

This time the door was opened by a very old woman who greeted him gruffly.

"Does Mademoiselle Aubertin live here?" he asked in French.

"Oui, Monsieur," answered the old woman, hesitantly. "Entrez!"

A second later the music stopped and Blanche appeared in the hall door.

"Who is it?" she asked.

"I have a message for you," replied Bob, with some amusement.

"A message—for me—from whom, Monsieur?" she said in surprise.

"A friend of mine, and of yours too, I believe, sends his compliments," continued Bob.

"But I don't understand, Monsieur," said the girl, puzzled.

"Oh, I wouldn't worry about it," said Bob with a smile. He thought to himself that with all his other faults, Warner had damned good taste. "He's on duty to-night over in Villaines, so he sent me in his place with a car, and I've come to take you for a drive if you're not too busy."

"Villaines? On duty? Oh yes, I see now. It's that officer who insulted me over there a few days ago. Now you want to insult me right here in my own home," cried Blanche. She was making a good deal of noise now, and was retreating into the drawing-room.

Bob saw at once that a terrible mistake had been made.

"Damn that Warner," he thought. But he couldn't let matters remain as they were. The girl was due some explanation, and by all means, an apology. So he followed her into the drawing-room and came face to face with Montie Jason, who was rushing out into the hall to learn the trouble. Both of them stood stock still—and glared at each other.

Bob was the first to speak. "What are you doing here, Sergeant?" he asked.

"I live here," replied Montie.

"Live here?" questioned the Lieutenant with sarcasm, glancing from him to the girl and then fixing his gaze on Montie again.

"Yes, sir!" replied Montie, with difficulty.

"Who is this girl?" demanded the officer. The sergeant's cool manner was irritating him—and the entire situation was certainly maddening to him—a Casper, from South Carolina.

"She is the daughter of the man who owns this house," replied Montie, with some asperity.

"What right have you to be living here? Enlisted men belong out in the billets—in the hay-lofts," shouted Bob. His anger was now at white heat, and he felt like striking this insolent nigger.

"You'll have to take that up with the Company Commander," replied Montie with confidence.

"Don't you dare talk back to me, you ———," Bob was having a terrible time. Before he could finish his sentence, Blache stepped up to him and addressed him directly.

"Monsieur, will you be good enough to leave my house."

"You'll hear more of this later," continued Bob, shaking his finger at Montie. He was furious. "I am Lieutenant Casper of the 2nd Battalion. What is your name and company?"

"Casper?" repeated Montie, "Casper, from South Carolina?"

"I'm glad you know whom you are dealing with," remarked the Lieutenant, with visible satisfaction. "What's your name?" he demanded again.

"Jason,—Montgomery Jason, Company 'L,'" he replied, indifferently.

"Oh, so you are the Montie Jason that I know about. Over here socializing with white women, are you?" Bob continued with a sneer.

For a moment Montie could say nothing. His voice choked. His mouth and tongue seemed parched. His bosom heaved. He had never been so angry in his life. He simply glared at Bob, like a bull before a matador.

"I see," he said at length, slowly and deliberately, between his teeth, "you carry your dirty southern prejudice with you everywhere you go."

"Listen to this, nigger," shouted Bob, "I had those chevrons put on your sleeve, and I'll be damned if I don't have them ripped off again!"

Miriam's weekly letter to Bob went unanswered that night.

XIV

It was evening. The sun had disappeared in a blaze of glory. Chameleon-like, the western sky was passing through a kaleidoscope of color. The big, fleecy clouds were streaked with pinks and reds. There were some in pale lavender, and still others in royal purple. The cultivated fields of deepening green rolled away into the distance and merged with the darkening sky. A white, winding road bisected the fields until it was lost in the rolling hills. Lazy, blue smoke curled skyward from the few farm-houses that dotted the surrounding country. A herd of goats grazed quietly in a meadow. All the world seemed at peace.

Private Jason lay at full length on a grassy knoll, chin in hand. For hours he had been there. He was only half conscious of the big, fleecy clouds in color, or of the green fields and the white road, or the hills, or the smoke, or the herd, or of the dusk itself. Montie was heart-sick. And the dull aching sensation in the core of him would not be silenced.

After the court-martial that afternoon he had started to walk. Two letters had been thrust in his hand as he left the company office. Mechanically, he put them into his pocket. He had not even stopped to remove the chevrons from his sleeves, as he had been sentenced to do. He just wanted to walk—and forget—and be alone. The road from Laval had brought him to this knoll. Perhaps he had been walking for an hour. At any rate, it was peaceful and quiet here. Perhaps if he stretched out on the grass he could absorb into his own soul some of the peace and calm of the country-side. Maybe he would stop thinking, and forget. But how could he forget? Could he ever forget that look of exultation that came over Casper's face when the sentence was pronounced? Could he ever erase from his memory the bitterness and scorn with which Casper had testified against him that afternoon? Or the venom in his voice?

Then his mind traveled to the war itself, to the destruction, and suffering, and death—to poor Jackson, who wanted a bottle of beer; to the corporal, who never reached the trench; to the hundreds of other black boys who had died and were rotting up there. For what good purpose, he asked himself. Came in answer all the high-sounding phrases that lull men's reason to sleep, and allow them to be led off like sheep to the slaughter—to make the world safe for democracy—war to end war—self determination for oppressed people. But they didn't mean black people. Oh no, black people don't count. They only count the dead. They are not even fit to be officers in their own regiment—not even non-commissioned officers if they are going to be friendly with white girls. Maybe Roscoe Simms was right after all. It was a white man's war. It would take more than war, and bullets, and death to wipe out race prejudice. What about minnies? Yes, big and loud as they are, it would take more than minnies to wipe out prejudice. Fellows like Casper would never change. They just hated black people, and that was all there was to it. It was a creed with them. Did Casper's mother ever teach him not to hate anybody. Then he thought of his own mother, and he remembered his letters.

In the failing light he read his mother's note. It was a prayer for his protection, and a Te Deum that he was still well and happy when she had last heard from him. How things had changed since then, he thought. And bitterness welled in his heart again—and the big, hot tears dropped on his mother's letter—and he longed for her comforting arms and consoling words.

The other letter was from Roscoe. It was the first word that Montie had received from him since he had been in France. Roscoe wrote briefly. He was expecting to be called in the draft any day. Teddy Burwell had already been conscripted and sent to a camp in Jersey. Jim Beasley's father was trying to get him into a medical school to escape the draft. Some of the other fellows who had been called were sent to labor battalions in Newport News. He had heard from Hazel Reed and she said that Miriam was teaching in a new school somewhere near her home—that it was a pretty good job. He hoped that Montie was well, and would see that peace was soon declared so that he, Roscoe, would not be called upon to kill Germans. And finally, the ever-recurring hope that Montie would return from the wars, a Major General.

Roscoe's letter unleashed another flood of thoughts. So they got Burwell, too. Poor Teddy. And there was Ted's mother. She was a widow and needed her boy. By the way, he had promised himself to write to Jackson's mother, and tell her how he died. The War Department would simply say that "Private James O. Jackson died in action." He hoped that the War Department would never have to write to his mother. It wasn't worth it—this dying for phrases. Prejudice was here to stay. Hell on Earth! That was it! That's what he had been trying to say all afternoon. Hell on Earth! And Miriam teaching in South Carolina! Oh yes, Casper came from South Carolina. Poor Miriam, having to teach in South Carolina. Hell on Earth! Suppose she'd have to meet up with a fellow like Casper. But she was lucky to be near her mother. He wished he was near to his mother. He never longed for her more in his life. By Jove, it was dark. It was time to get back. Back to the hay-loft. And lie awake, thinking some more. Didn't this maddening thinking ever end? Minnies would end it. No, no, machine guns were better. There were more of them.

XV

"Well, heah we is agin. The war ain' ovah."

"Not by a damn sight," commented Montie, as a screaming shell passed over the moving column of trucks, and fell three or four kilometers behind them. "They're shelling that town we passed through a little while ago. We'll get ours later."

"Damn right we will," was the reply, "but them two weeks rest sho' was sweet."

The regiment had entrained the previous day, and was now in a new sector. The outfit had reached the rail-head at noon. Since then they had been traveling in trucks along roads hidden by dried, brown camouflage. All the afternoon they had been passing pile after pile of shells covered with painted canvas, or hidden in the edge of the woods. Artillery-men were busy getting big guns into emplacements. Horses and mules, dead in the cause of democracy, were strung out all along the way. Caches of stores of all kinds were easily visible from the trucks. A constant stream of traffic, all moving forward, cluttered up the road.

"Looks like big business," remarked a sergeant, who rode beside Montie on the tail-board.

"A new drive up ahead, I guess," Montie answered.

Just about dark they left the trucks and settled down for the night in a prepared camping area in a patch of pine. About 2 A. M. they were aroused.

"We're moving up! Prepare to pull out in ten minutes!"

Dawn found the 2nd Battalion in a support line of trenches, and the 3rd Battalion hidden in a sheltered wood not far behind them. The front was unusually quiet.

"The lull before the storm," thought Montie, as he prepared to snatch a little sleep under a low-hanging bow.

Late in the afternoon Lieutenant Mahoney assembled his platoon.

"We're taking part in a big drive which gets under way day after to-morrow at dawn," he began. "This regiment has been given a very important sector because of our fine showing in that other engagement. We've got a reputation to live up to now. Our objective in this drive is a ridge of hills overlooking a valley about four kilometers away—a big assignment. The 2nd Battalion will relieve the French in the front lines to-night, and will form the first waves of the attack. We'll move up and take their places in support, to-night. Our battalion will furnish the succeeding waves of attack. I'm telling you this now, because I may not get the chance to have you all assembled together again. We've got to fight, and fight like hell. That's all."

The dawn of the day after to-morrow finally arrived— warm and cloudy. It had drizzled slightly off and on during the night. The front was nervous. Star shells and Very lights were more frequent than usual. The trigger fingers of the machine gunners reflected their own nervousness. The Germans knew that an attack was imminent. They always knew. The French and Americans were afraid of raids for prisoners. Every little noise or movement brought down a burst of machine gun fire; each side retaliated with its own machine guns, and then when affairs got too active, the artillery would open up, to quiet things down. But dawn came at last.

Suddenly a roar deafened. It announced to the Germans that the long-heralded offensive was on. It notified the French and Americans, crouched in miles and miles of trenches, that the zero hour had come. The earth quaked and vibrated from the detonation of a thousand unseen guns. Then as the barrage crept forward, the infantry debouched from their trenches, following the falling shells as closely as they dared. The Germans waited in their concrete dug-outs deep in the bowels of the earth. When the shells stopped falling, they rushed up and attempted to man their machine guns to stop the advancing waves of infantry.

All morning, however, the advance kept on. Montie could see that the resistance was slight. The enemy was evidently withdrawing behind a certain prepared line. The 2nd Battalion was pushing ahead on the heels of the Boche. The 3rd Battalion was backing up the 2nd.

About noon the advance came to a sudden halt. The battalions had now come in clear view of the ridge of hills that formed their objective. This ridge had a commanding view of the plains on each side of it. It was evident that no troops could remain long in either plain with that ridge in the hands of opposing forces. The Germans had withdrawn behind the ridge, and were prepared to make a stand there. From their commanding position on the hill-crest, the Boche swept the plain below with an incessant and withering fire. In addition to this, their artillery had the exact range and was showering a rain of shrapnel and high explosive shells on the advancing infantry.

The 2nd Battalion was compelled to stop, and take cover in the former German trenches which they were passing over. It was sheer suicide to remain above ground. How-ever, it was not difficult to find cover, for the surface of the ground was covered with trenches and shell-holes. But the advance was definitely halted—and the objective had not been reached.

Like an awakening giant, the French artillery opened up once more, and concentrated its fire on the ridge. Under cover of this fire, the 2nd Battalion was ordered to advance again. The machine gun fire was not nearly so devastating as it had been, but the Boche artillery was raining shells upon the exposed infantry.

Montie's battalion which had started out in support, had moved up rapidly, and was now practically merged with the decimated 2nd Battalion. Montie had thus far come through unscathed. He was beginning to feel that he had a charmed life. His buddies were going down all around him, but he kept plugging ahead from trench to trench, and from hole to hole. A thin line was gradually approach-ing the upward slope of the ridge. From the shelter of a small gully Montie saw the ragged line of the remnants of the 2nd Battalion laboriously making its way up the slope. He could see that they were protected now from the hell-ish artillery fire that was falling in the plain where he was. He could also see, however, that they were exposed to the rifle and machine gun fire from the trenches at the top of the ridge.

Gradually, Montie made his way to the foot of the slope.

The Boche fire from the ridge had increased to such an extent now, that further progress was impossible. The 2nd Battalion was completely stopped half-way up the hill. They needed help or they would be forced to drop back themselves to the foot of the slope. The 3rd Battalion, in support, was moving up as rapidly as possible. But nothing could live long on that hill-side. A few of the supporting waves reached the advance line of the 2nd Battalion, but even this was not enough to continue the advance over open ground to the crest of the hill. Still more help would have to be sent.

Montie Jason was among the few who reached the advance position held by the 2nd Battalion. A leaden hail was sweeping the slope of the hill. He jumped into a trench as a burst of bullets tore up the spot that he had just left. Carefully, he surveyed his position. He saw at a glance that it was useless to go further up the slope because there was absolutely no cover between him and the crest. Besides, only a handful of men had reached this advanced position, and until additional help arrived it was suicidal to move, either forward or backward.

On the other hand, he knew that the Germans were content behind their strongly entrenched ridge, and would certainly not make any attempt to dislodge the two battalions before night. By night, he knew that the 1st Battalion and the French would come to their rescue. So for the time being, he felt safe, although he did feel a bit lonely in that big trench all by himself. He decided to remain quiet so as not to attract the attention of the Boche up the hill.

Suddenly he caught a sound in the trench to his right. He leaped into attention. The bay of the trench obscured his view. He listened.

"Sounds like a groan," he thought, "some poor devil, I guess."

However, he decided to return to his lookout on the fire-step. But the groaning continued, louder, too. It worried Montie.

"Maybe I can give him a drink, anyhow," he thought.

Carefully he edged around the bay in the trench, taking pains to keep his own head down below the parapet. He stopped aghast. Two soldiers, both apparently dead, were lying heads down in the trench with their feet sticking up on the sandbags. Underneath the two of them, was an officer, flat on his back, in the bottom of the trench. It was clear to Montie that a machine gun had caught all three of them at once, as they were making a dash for the trench.

It was the officer who was groaning. Slowly and carefully, Montie moved the two soldiers to one side. They were dead. Then he knelt quickly by the wounded officer, raised the head so as to remove the helmet which partially obscured his face, and recognized Bob Casper.

Montie's first impulse was to throw him back on the ground, and return to his lookout in the other trench. The wounded man was regaining consciousness now, and his groaning was becoming more pitiful. "God, I can't leave him like this," Montie whispered to himself, in a husky voice.

He took out his own canteen and raised it to Bob's lips. Then he moistened a khaki handkerchief and swabbed the officer's forehead and temples. After unbuttoning the shirt at the neck, Montie gave him a hasty examination to find the wound. It was the left leg, shattered just above the knee by at least a half dozen bullets. The blood was still oozing, and Montie guessed that Casper had fainted from loss of blood. Quickly he devised a rough tourniquet from the handkerchief and applied it to the leg. Bob winced. Montie looked up.

"Am I hurting you?" he asked.

"God it's killing me," replied the wounded officer, in agony.

Montie propped him up in what he thought might be the most comfortable position. There was nothing else to do. Bob lay there with his eyes closed, groaning. Montie decided to survey his position again. He eased his head above the parapet and took a hasty look. Things had quieted down considerably. He noticed that his own battalion and the remainder of the 2nd Battalion had virtually retired to the foot of the slope, to await further reinforcements. The Germans were satisfied that no immediate attack was pending, so they were utilizing the lull to strengthen their own position. They knew that the next onslaught would not come before dusk. Although he was way out in front of his own lines, Montie knew that he was perfectly safe. All he had to do was to remain quiet for the rest of the afternoon and then rejoin his outfit at dark.

Bob had stopped groaning now. He was thoroughly conscious. Montie sat opposite on the fire-step watching him. Bob opened his eyes. He looked hard at Montie, then the light of recognition shone in his eyes.

"You're Jason, aren't you?" he asked slowly.

"Yes, but I wouldn't try to talk, or even think, if I were you," replied Montie.

"Can they hear us?" whispered Bob.

"No. But you're too weak to talk."

"But I want to thank you," he murmured.

"Does your leg feel better?"

"God yes, but it's still bleeding. Where are the others?"

"What others?"

"The battalion."

"They're down the hill."

"Are we up here alone?"

"All alone," was the answer.

Bob closed his eyes again. The talking exhausted him. As Montie sat and looked at him, a maze of thoughts kept whirling pell-mell through his brain. This was the man who had taken shelter behind his official rank to insult him in Blanche Aubertin's house. This same man had preferred charges against him, that had caused him to be court-martialed and reduced to the ranks. And only because he, Montie, was a Negro—and Casper was a southern white man. The more he thought, the more furious he became.

Suddenly, Bob began to groan again. "God, I can't stand it," he cried, "it's killing me."

Montie's anger turned to pity. "Lord, but he's suffering—and he's bleeding to death, too," he thought.

Slowly Montie raised his head again and surveyed the ground and the distance between him and the foot of the slope. Then he ran his eye along the plain across which they had come. He knew that by now the Medical Corps had established dressing stations down in the German dugouts which had fallen into their hands. He turned again and looked at the wounded man in the bottom of the trench. He was suffering untold misery.

"They can't save his leg, but they can save his life, if I can get him down this hill," he thought.

Like a streak he was in the trench beside the Lieutenant. "Take another drink," he said quickly.

"What are you going to do?" breathed Bob.

"I'm going to get you out of here, where you can get attention," answered Montie, resting his rifle against the sand-bags.

"I won't last much longer, and the risk is too great," protested Bob.

"You leave that to me," replied Montie.

"God, but you're a prince," whispered Bob. Then with his eyes closed, he added, very slowly, "war isn't the only hell that I've been through lately."

"Don't worry about that now. Here we go," said Montie, cheerfully.

Placing his arms under Bob, he raised him horizontally and slowly slipped him over the parapet. Then he ran quickly along the inside of the trench and crawled out at another place. Lying as flat on the ground as he could, he edged his way between some sand-bags until he reached the wounded man. Carefully he turned Bob over on his face, with his head pointed down the hill. Then he slipped his arm around Bob's waist, and lying flat, face down, started to crawl.

Rat-tat-tat broke out a maxim gun at the top of the hill. Montie and Bob hugged the earth. But the bullets went whining down into the plain where somebody had unconsciously exposed himself. Encouraged they kept snaking forward. Every now and then Montie would whisper a word of cheer to his wounded companion. Bob remained conscious. The excitement kept him going. He dragged himself along with Montie, trying to forget the pain.

Finally they reached a rain gully and Montie knew that they were completely hidden from the crest. He stopped to rest. Again he gave Bob a drink, and moistened his forehead and temples. The Lieutenant smiled at him weakly.

"Not much farther now," said Montie, "let's try again."

Once more they set out on their slow, painful journey. Twice more they stopped to rest.

"How much farther?" gasped Bob.

"Just a little way," whispered Montie.

Again they resumed the struggle. Then came a sudden riveting of maxims. Two bodies slumped as one.

They found them the next morning, face downward, their arms about each other, side by side.

Stories from the *Crisis*

Private Walker Goes Patrolling

Jerry Walker did not know what it was all about. He made no secret of that. To him, the war was somebody's else business—and he had always been told to mind his own. He had a very remote idea that somewhere across the river and out beyond Memphis, somebody was having a war. He would have none of it. He hated a fight.

But the man at the Court House in Cotton Plant thought differently. With a heavy heart and a heavier foot Jerry Walker dragged himself into Camp Pike. Elijah couldn't have been any more bewildered when he landed in Heaven. The rows and rows of little wooden barracks awed him. Marching soldiers and barking non-coms terrified him. Hustle, bustle, everywhere. Jerry was just plumb scared to death.

The next chapter in Jerry's life might have been entitled "Six Weeks" or "From Farm-hand to Dough-boy." Jerry made a bum soldier. Naturally as aggressive as the family cow, one other factor contributed to his unhappy lot—the top-sergeant.

"Memphis Bill," otherwise known as First Sergeant William Dade, was a born soldier, if soldiering meant the love of a fight. Memphis Bill was known to pack a punch. Beale Street could testify to that. Six foot four in his stocking feet, arms dangling to his knees, voice sounding like a brass horn—thundering, threatening, cursin', what a top-sergeant he did make. Bill was a man among men. He also

Originally printed in the Crisis, *June 1930.*

thought that he was a man among women, too. As a matter of fact, Bill had only one real weakness, women. He was even more proud of his charm and grace among women, than he was of his strength and prowess among the men of his acquaintance.

Memphis Bill had taken a hearty dislike to Jerry Walker at first sight. Deep in his subconscious mind, Bill had the feeling that somewhere before he had met this same Jerry—and there was something peculiarly distasteful to Bill about the thought. He felt that he knew this "aukard, lazy, good-fer-nothin' stiff" as he characterized Jerry, but for the life of him, he couldn't figure out why or how or where he had ever "met up wid de laks of sich trash befor'."

"Whar yo' frum, sojer?" he had roared at Jerry on the occasion of their first meeting in the mess hall.

"Awk'nsaw," was Jerry's laconic reply, and from then on Bill knew that he disliked Jerry.

Not long after, Bill had suddenly jumped up from a huge boulder on which he had been resting by the side of the road and marched straight over to Jerry, who had seized the few minutes of rest on his first practice hike, to remove his shoes.

"Sojer, yo' ever been'n Memfis?" he had demanded of Jerry.

"Once't," came the meager, disinterested response, and Bill had walked back slowly to his boulder shaking his head and mumbling to himself.

The top-sergeant's dislike for Jerry showed itself in many forms. Poor Jerry found himself a member of every disagreeable detail. There was no end of kitchen police for him. When stumps on the drill ground had to be grubbed, his was the first name called. He never was assigned to guard duty in the middle of the week, only on Saturdays and Sundays, when the rest of the outfit was off duty. Sergeant William Dade was relentless in his petty persecution of Private Jerry Walker.

Jerry, on the other hand, didn't exactly fall in love with

the top-sergeant at first sight, either. But for that matter he didn't like the lieutenants, or the captain, or the army, or the war. He hated a fight, although he was no coward. He kept repeating to himself that the war was none of his affair, and he detested everything connected with it. And because he hated the war and the army and the officers and the details, most of the top-sergeant's persecution was absolutely lost on Jerry. Since he was there against his will anyhow, what difference did it make what he was called upon to do. Kitchen police was no more disagreeable than marching for hours up and down the dusty old drill ground, and never going anywhere. Just marching, marching, marching—and never arriving! Grubbing stumps was a pleasure compared to the ridiculous tactics of flopping down on your stomach behind the stumps and stupidly clicking the trigger on your gun as though you were shooting at somebody. And guard duty was no trouble—it was a relief—a relief to get away from everybody, and be by himself in some lonely patch of woods down by the railroad station, or way out by the highway gate where only a few stragglers would pass all day.

So most of Memphis Bill's scheming hostility to Jerry went for naught. The sergeant listened in vain for the first word of complaint or the first sign of dissatisfaction on the part of his victim—and Jerry's total indifference just further—infuriated him.

"I wish he'd open his mouf, so I could mash it," Bill would sigh to himself. But Jerry never opened it.

"Sergeant, I want you to take a detail of four men and explore the abandoned communication trench running out in front of the Company sector. Wait until it gets dark. Don't go too far; but go far enough to contact the enemy barbed wire."

"Yas suh, Cap'n," spoke up Sergeant Bill Dade, and saluting, turned on his heel and strode thoughtfully away.

"Detail, detail," he kept mumbling to himself, "hyar's whar I fixes dat pol'cat frum Awk'nsaw."

"Co'pral, git me two o' yo' men right quick, an' hav'em repo't to mah dugout at once't," commanded the top-sergeant to the first corporal he could find.

"Hey, yo', sojer!" roared Bill a few minutes later, stepping up behind Private Jerry Walker who leaned absently against the parapet of a trench, looking out into space, wondering what it was all about.

"Git yo'self t'gidder an' cum 'long wid me—stanin' dar lak Ston'all Jackson! What yo' starin' at, anyhow?"

"Nothin'," drawled Jerry, looking up from his reverie, and glaring into the scowling face above him.

Bill's brow darkened, and he glowered at Jerry with an evil eye. That crushing right fist itched nervously. "Not now," he mumbled to himself, "mah time'll cum."

"Sta'k dem rifles hyar in dis dugout! Whar yo' alls t'inks yo' alls gwine—Berlin?" shouted Sergeant Dade, as he lined up his patrol for final instructions and inspection.

The sun had dropped hazily behind the wooded peaks of the Vosges several hours before, and a cloudy sky gave promise of one of those inky, pitch-black nights that this sector was noted for. Nights that seemed to be hewn from ebony itself. Nights on which it was impossible to distinguish friend from foe. Nights on which it was just as dangerous to move around behind your own lines as it was behind the enemy's.

"Hurry 'em along, Sergeant, it's getting late, and it's black as Hell out here," came a voice down the steps of the dug-out.

"Yas suh, Lootenan', cumin'," sang out Bill from the depths below. His spirits were rising now. He sniffed a fight. His huge hob-nailed feet literally pawed the ground. Memphis Bill was rarin' to go.

"Now Co'pral, yo' an' yo' two sojers will git into dat trencht as soon as we gits pas' our wire. Mak' yo' alls way ahaid in singl' file tru de trencht 'till yo' all gits to de

Boshes wire, an' den wait dar fo' me. Me an' Big Boy hyar frum Awk'nsaw'll crawl along each side o' de trencht, an' ef we sees any trubl' ahaid, we'll signal to yo' all down in de trencht fer to stop. Git me?" And with that he cast a triumphant glance in the direction of Private Jerry Walker. But as usual, the glance was lost for want of a receiver. Jerry wasn't even looking. He was barely listening. Certainly he wasn't thinking. He was just there, no more, no less. It wasn't his war—and he hated a fight.

"No shootin'," was the sergeant's final order, "ef we meets up wid any Boshes use yer fistes, and dem trencht knifes o' yourn. Shootin' never did nobody no good, nohow. Use yer fistes!" With that he led the way up out of the dug-out into the inky blackness of the night.

"Feld," a muffled voice whispered in a strange tone not three feet from where Memphis Bill lay flat on his stomach out there in the ebony night.

"Maus," came back the other half of the pass word from out of the blackness. Bill's big heart was bumping against the ground as his eyes searched in vain for the enemy patrol that he knew was passing through them.

If he could only see. If he only knew where the rest of his patrol had gone to. Where was that big stiff from Arkansas hiding? Where was the trench? If he only knew what time it was. Gee he'd hate to go back and face the Captain and the Lieutenant—and the men. How they'd snicker and laugh behind his back. He, Memphis Bill, world-beater, lost—hopelessly, helplessly lost. His patrol lost. Maybe captured by now. Hell! What a big bum they'd call him. It must be nearly daybreak. How long had he been groping around out there in that black tomb? Which way was forward and which way was backward. These and a million similar thoughts were torturing the mind of that big hulk as it lay there helpless in the pitch dark.

Bill was beaten. Just once before in his life he had been

beaten, and there was nothing to do but take it. He would have to stay where he was until morning. "Dam' sich nights," he swore under his breath.

Suddenly the sergeant became aware of a movement near him. He strained his eyes in vain. He strained every nerve to pierce the mystery of that veil of night. He lay perfectly still—motionless. He was tense. Bill was on guard, ready to spring at a split-second notice, just like a big black panther. Was it the enemy patrol returning? Was it one of his own men? Was he still in No-Man's Land, or was he actually within the enemy lines?

"Whar d'Hell am I?" he kept asking himself.

But nothing appeared out of the darkness for him to spring upon, and gradually the sergeant relaxed to await the coming of dawn. The rest of the night passed quietly.

Gradually, Sergeant Dade began to recognize objects about him. Carefully, quietly, he reconnoitered his position. Quickly he realized that he couldn't stay where he was much longer. He found himself perched on top of a grassy knoll that was plainly visible from the surrounding hills, some of which were less than two hundred yards away. But the factor that bothered the patrol leader most at that moment, was which way led to safety. Now that it was getting light and he could see, he was ready to go, but he had no place to go.

In that particular sector in the Vosges, battle-lines were not clearly defined. Both sides had entrenched themselves at strategic points throughout the heavily wooded hills, and were satisfied to adopt a policy of watchful waiting. It was known as a quiet sector. New troops were sent there by both sides to learn the art of war under the most favorable circumstances. Patrolling was the most active form of encounter. In some places the mythical lines were a half a mile apart, at other points they came as close as one hundred and fifty yards, depending solely on the nature of the terrain.

That's why Bill Dade was so completely lost. He couldn't

tell one hill from another. "Why doan dey hang out a flag or sumptin' so a guy c'n tell whar he's at," thought Bill as the hopelessness of his situation dawned upon him with the morning light. He failed to recognize a single land-mark that would give him the slightest clue to his where-abouts. But he had to get off that knoll.

In one direction the knoll sloped gently to a large open field that evidently had been used as pasture land before the war. For Bill to venture forth into that open field would have been disastrous if any of the surrounding hills were occupied by the Boche. Snipers, who were constantly on the lookout high up in the tree-tops, would spot him as soon as the morning haze lifted from the valley. You never could tell in those hills and woods when snipers were taking aim on you—and since it was a one-shot game, they rarely missed. In the opposite direction the knoll sloped much more abruptly, and was practically covered by a growth of young pine. This side of the hill had at one time or another been under shell fire, as a number of broken trees and ragged shell-holes testified. At the foot of the slope about a hundred feet distant was the dried bed of a brook, from which the steep sides of another thickly wooded hill arose. The sergeant saw that this dried stream bed at the foot of both slopes, offered him the best shelter for the pres-ent. Gathering his six foot four together, Bill set out on his hands and knees, moving cautiously and silently. When he reached the foot of the slope his eye fell upon a small section of the bank that had been undercut by the force of the water years ago. Exposed roots of overhanging trees in front of this section of the bank furnished ideal support for the honeysuckle and other vines that formed a perfect mesh across the opening of the undercut bank. Here was a perfectly screened cave. Sergeant Dade felt for the first time in many hours that luck had come his way. He would keep watch from this hiding place until dusk, hoping that by then something would happen to give him some idea of where he was in respect to the war.

Once more he resumed his crawling tactics. Finally he reached the vines hanging in front of the cave. Just as he was about to part them and peer in, he was struck by the sound of a familiar voice from within.

"Cum in befo' yo' brings de whole army wid yo'."

There sat Private Jerry Walker of Arkansas, atop a huge round stone.

"Fer cryin' in de sink!" was Bill's hushed exclamation.

"Whar's de Co'pral?" he excitedly continued.

"I dunno."

"Whar's dem sojers o' his'n?"

"I dunno."

"Whar's dat ar trencht we cum out in?"

"I dunno."

"Yo' doan know much, does yo'?" Bill added sarcastically.

"No, but I ain't los'."

At that moment the dull roar of a squadron of planes overhead brought both men sharply to the realization that this was neither the time nor the place for argument.

"What I wants t' know mos'," continued the sergeant, some minutes later, in an almost friendly manner, "is which one o' dem hills is de one we cum over las' night?"

"Dar it stan's," nodded Jerry decisively, in the direction of a sparsely covered hill about a couple of hundred yards across the valley.

"How yo' know?" eagerly spoke up the gent from Memphis, parting the vines and peering out enthusiastically.

"Cuz I staid up atop o' it all night, 'till I crawls down hyar dis mornin'."

"Well, fool, whatcher cum dis way fo'; why yo' didn't crawl back d'udder way whar we cums frum?"

"Cuz I seen one o' dem Boshes wand'rin' roun' out dar— look lak t' me he was los', too—an' cuz I wasn't after gittin' mix'd up wid 'im, I cums on dis way 'till it gits dark, den I'se gwine ba'k."

This was the longest speech that Jerry Walker had made

since he joined the armed forces of his Uncle Samuel. It seemed to leave him exhausted for he lapsed into a grave-like silence. The sergeant, satisfied now that he would be able to make his way back to his outfit soon after dark, stretched himself out at full length on the ground, and gradually went off to sleep. The day wore on uneventfully. Bill slept off and on, while Jerry kept watch.

Finally, refreshed by several hours of sleep and a little water from his canteen, Memphis Bill aroused himself. He was in better spirits now. He cast his gaze in the direction of his roommate who was as motionless as the stone on which he sat. Bill felt grateful. He knew that he owed his chance of getting back safely to his outfit, to this same soldier for whom he had developed such a strong dislike.

"After all," thought Bill, "he ain't never done nuthin' t'me."

"When we gits ba'k to de States," said the sergeant in the friendliest voice, "I wants yo' to stop off wid me in Memfis an' meet sum o' mah gals."

"I doan lak Memfis," replied Jerry breaking his long silence.

"Watcher know 'bout Memfis?" queried Bill, his voice still friendly, and his eyes sparkling at the thought of the figure he'd cut when he returned to Beale Street in his First Sergeant's uniform and his swagger stick.

"Been dar once't, an' gits into a fite. Ain' never gwine dar no mo'!"

"Tell me 'bout it, Big Boy," pleaded Bill sympathetically.

And then Jerry, in a low voice, after some hesitation, told the story of his one trip to Memphis. And Bill sat there on the floor of their cave looking up at him in wide-eyed amazement.

Jerry told how he had gone to Memphis on an excursion boat, one Sunday about a year before the war. How he had wandered about the big city most of the day, sight-seeing, and finally wound up late in the afternoon in a Beale Street cafe. The place had been crowded with hungry excursionists, who were trying to get something to eat before the boat started back on its trip down the river. Seated atop a high stool at the lunch counter, Jerry was suddenly startled by the shrill scream of a woman, followed by the sound of blows to the accompaniment of curses and shouts. Looking about him in dismay, he realized that a fight had started at a table in the corner and was rapidly progressing in his direction. As the crowd of non-combatants gave way before the approach of the fighters, Jerry from his perch on the stool, could see that three of the excursionists appeared to be battling with a huge man, who seemed to be getting the better of the scrap, in spite of the odds against him. Jerry's heart had been made sick by this desecration of the Sabbath—and he hated a fight anyhow. The huge man kept his opponents at bay as he slowly backed his way toward the door. Both fists were lashing out skull-crushing blows, and his opponents continued their attacks from a respectful distance. Finally the battlers had reached a place near where Jerry was perched at the counter. The huge fighter's back was almost touching Jerry. He made a terrific lunge at his nearest assailant and floored him with a hay-making right uppercut. But in so doing he lost his own footing on the greasy floor and slipped to his knees, almost under Jerry's stool. Then Jerry told how he had been seized with a sudden, mad frenzy to end this disgusting fight. Looking about him, he grabbed with both hands a huge earthen crock half full of waffle batter and brought it down with all his force upon the head of the massive fighter, who was just about to rise off one knee.

Momentarily dazed by this sudden attack from a new quarter, and partially blinded by the messy batter that engulfed him from the broken crock, the giant fighter was easily subdued by his remaining two opponents who were still on their feet. Once inside of that deadly right, they flung their combined weight against him and thrashed him within an inch of his life. When Jerry left the cafe several minutes later, they were loading this Colossus of Clout into a hospital ambulance.

"'Twasn't dat I had anyt'ing agin' dat man," Jerry concluded, "I never seen him befo' nor sence, but I jest nateraly hates a fite, an' I wanted fer to stop dem frum fitin'."

Sergeant William Dade sat through this recital absolutely speechless. He seemed to be drinking in every word that fell from Jerry's lips. Toward the end, he sat rigid and fixed, like a bird in the charm of a snake. That clenched, crushing right fist itched nervously. He remembered that fight perfectly. He could taste that batter yet!

Suddenly there was a sound just outside their hiding place. Yes—another and another. They could hear the breaking of small twigs, but they couldn't see anything. Inside the cave was the stillness of death. Neither man dared move. Jerry sat on the edge of his stone. Bill was on his hands and knees, ready to spring—like a wild cat. He was afraid that the thumping of his heart would give them away. He tried to see through the labyrinth of vines, but there was nothing to see. He was just about to speak when a huge frame darkened the front of their cave. From his place on the ground Sergeant Dade could see the shoes and the leggings of the man standing not two feet away from him. He was a Boche.

One second's reflection was all that Memphis Bill needed. He would carry that Boche back alive to his outfit if he had to whip the whole German army one by one. It would absolve him from his sin of getting lost on patrol. It would restore his standing with the Lieutenant, with the Captain, and above all, with the men. It would make him a hero instead of a goat.

So without the slightest consideration for his companion, Bill made up his mind. He waited a moment until the soldier moved away from the cave entrance, and then he suddenly emerged from his hiding. As he straightened up he was confronted with the biggest man that he had ever seen in his life. The German was dumbfounded. He was also unarmed. And as his enemy made no effort to draw the automatic that dangled from his belt, the Teuton saw that he had a chance, and he cleared for action. Quick as a flash he sized up his opponent; he realized from Bill's bulk and the determined look in his eyes that this was no mean adversary. So he was prepared for the terrific right uppercut that just missed his chin by an eyelash. Like lightning itself, he whipped over a left hook that caught the astounded Bill flush on the jaw. The gent from Memphis shook the cob-webs from his brain as it slowly dawned upon him that he had met more than his match. So there they stood in that quiet, peaceful valley, in the gathering dusk, toe to toe, the Bavarian butcher and the stevedore from Memphis, trading punches, blow for blow. Bill realized that the Boche could take it and the Boche could give it, too. The German wondered what kind of animal this was that could kick like a mule with his right arm and grin like an ape at the hardest blows. The battle raged in front of the cave, and Jerry crouched behind the vines. He hated a fight.

Bill was giving ground now. One eye was partially closed, and he was bleeding profusely from the nose. His adversary realized this and was trying desperately for a knockout. He shot a wicked left to Bill's chin that sent him reeling and groggy, but the German slipped on the treacherous gravel in front of the cave. He went down on one knee almost under the stone on which Jerry was sitting behind the vines.

Private Jerry Walker was suddenly seized with a mad frenzy to end this disgusting fight. Quick as a flash he thrust his arm through the vines and came down with all his force upon the unprotected Bavarian skull with the butt end of an army automatic. The huge frame crumpled in a heap. Jerry had stopped the fight.

"Well, Big Boy, I gess we's quits," was Sergeant Dade's only comment. As usual, this was lost on Jerry.

Shortly after dark the news spread like wildfire through the Company sector—battalion headquarters, five miles back, got it—Sergeant "Memphis Bill" Dade had stayed all night and all day in the German lines, and had just returned, dragging a two hundred and fifty pound Boche with him. But to every proffered congratulation, Bill had only the one laconic reply, "Giv' it to muh buddie hyar from Awk'nsaw!"

Goats, Wildcats and Buffalo

For four nights the relief had been going on. The feverish activity would begin at dark and continue until the break of day. During the day nobody stirred. The wooded hills held the secret.

A solitary goat-herd and his flock were the only living things in all that great expanse of mountain country, that defied the gods of war. Back on a green, hilly slope behind the artillery emplacements the flock grazed peacefully every day, tended by their grizzled owner. Some of the goats were in full view of the Boche across the valley; part of the herd was always hidden by a pine-covered hill.

This was a quiet sector—more or less of a rest zone for tired Boche troops, and a training area for Yanks. German ammunition was low. German artillery was worn out. There were too many other uses for it than just goats. Besides, one never stirred up anything on a quiet sector. It was an unwritten law. Consequently, the goats grazed peacefully day after day, oblivious of the tired Boche or nervous Yank. From the German trenches the flock must have looked like little white stars on a green theatre curtain.

One by one the units of the "Wildcat" Division from the Carolinas were replaced by the black battalions of the "Buffaloes." Each night for the past week the black troops, from a widely scattered area, were concentrating toward the front in their new sector. They came by train, then

Originally printed in the Crisis, *March 1932.*

truck, and finally by long night marches. During the day they hid away in the heavy pine forests in the foot-hills of the Vosges. Unfriendly planes would not carry the news that America assembled her black battalions in the Haute Marne sector.

In the dead of night—in the solemn, inky darkness of those mountain strongholds, black replaced white. Sound and echo carried far in those hills. Never a voice was raised above a whisper—never an unnecessary word. Never an order, where a push or shove might do. Every foot-fall was guarded with the utmost care. Almost on tip-toe the thin black lines filed in, as the single white lines moved out.

During the day the white goats grazed on in full view of the Boche.

For four nights everything went well. On the fifth night the relief was to be concluded. The few remaining units completed their exchange early. The last "Buffalo" had taken the place of the final "Wildcat." Company command-ers finished their check-ups and turn-overs, wished each other well, and breathed a sigh of relief. Long before dawn the last column of "Wildcats" had disappeared far down the valley, well satisfied that the Boche had been completely tricked. Officers and men extended congratulations to one another. Yankee brains!

Back up on the front the "Buffalo" Division was equally well satisfied. Not a man had been lost in the relief. Thirty thousand men had moved in and out, and the enemy was completely confounded. Suppose that they had been aware of the relief. The Boche could have annihilated the Divi-sion in those pitch black hills. Miles back, the Division Commander penned an order to be sent up to the entire outfit at daybreak. Congratulations were in order.

Morning dawned at last.

What were those peculiar, indiscernible markers over the German lines? They had not been there the night before. In the dim morning light they looked like signs. Signs? On the front? "What the hell!" roared a top-ser-

geant. The light was becoming stronger now. They were
signs! All along the front, at regular intervals. The words
were blurred. But the light was getting better all the time.
The news flashed along the Yankee front. Every eye was
strained to read. Yes, they were printed in English. Finally
the light was strong enough. Everybody could read:

"GOOD-BYE WILDCATS—WELCOME BUFFALOES."

A hand-full of black goats grazed peacefully in full view
of the German trenches. The white ones were hidden from
view by the pine-covered hill.

Still Five More

"Yas, suh! Ole Job had it, an' Marfa an' Mary had it, an' Peter done thought he had it, too. An' it's writ dat lessen you an' me an' all de res' ob us is got it, we's jes po' los' chil'ren."

"Amen, Zeke!"

"Wid out faith in de Lawd Jesus, all us Niggers be still in slavery right now," continued Zeke.

"Sho' nuff?"

"Cose! It's done writ dat faith'll move mountains."

"Ah's a Christian an' all lak dat, but ah 'fess ah doan unnerstan' 'bout dis heah faith," inserted another, slowly.

Zeke was on him like a bird of prey. "You is jes a doubtin' Thomas what ain't nebber gwine git nowhar's. How come you reckon us niggers done taken dat white man prisoner, lessen we had faith?"

The white man, proof of faith, turned his head and cast a look of penetrating scorn upon his Bible-quoting captors. He merely issued a mouthful of tobacco juice, but it was enough to quell, momentarily anyhow, the running conversation in the squad that had made him prisoner just a short while before.

Noon—and the August sun beat down ferociously on a thick clump of dust covered bushes and four grizzled horsemen peering out from behind them. There were two

Originally printed in the Crisis, *February 1934.*

roads to watch—the Warrenton Turnpike, and the narrow, unfrequented road winding over to Thoroughfare Gap in Bull Run Mountain, over which the little group of cavalrymen had just ridden in. The bushes, located at the road-fork, afforded a fair view of both roads, and an excellent hiding place.

"Yo' all doan reckon all them Yanks cleared outta heah las' night?" questioned one of the four men. His voice, coarse and low, vibrated with doubt.

"The pu'pose of this heah patrol is to fin' out jes that, 'cordin' to mah way o' reckonin'," spoke up another of the group.

"We ain't see a damn Yankee sence we lef' the Valley," added one of the others.

"This perticular country's been right lousy with 'em. Doan see how all uv 'em coulda got pas' heah so soon."

"Cose it's heaps longer the way we come—through the Valley."

"We been ridin' right smart, though."

"It's a good ten mile from heah to Warr'nton, an' another twen'y mile to the river."

"An mos' o' them Yankees is hikin'."

"They ain't losin' no time, though, them Yanks. Pope 'spicions by now Ole Stonewall's trying to git betwixt him an' Wash'nton."

"Ah wouldn' be none su'prised ef it ain't a damn Yankee from heah clean to Warr'nton."

"Reckon so, too, but we'll soon fin' that out. We's come fur enough."

"Too fur, mebbe."

"Seems lak we orter dismount heah an' give these animals a res'. When we leaves heah yo' all may be in a hellfire hurry." He chuckled at his own humor.

The little group followed this suggestion without comment. Each gave attention to his own mount. But their vigilance never relaxed. Slowly the sun moved toward the hills of the Shenandoah.

Suddenly, as one man, they vaulted back into their saddles. The sounds were distinct. But the bend in the road prevented them from seeing anything but the cloud of dust over the Turnpike. Each of the horsemen gripped the mouth of his mount firmly with one hand. There could be no neighing now. The noise on the Pike increased rapidly. The voices became more excited as they grew clearer.

"Sounds lak Rebs," whispered one of the patrol. Knitted brows and confused countenances showed that they were all harboring the same notion.

"Yankees never made no racket lak that, marchin' 'long a road," breathed one of them.

"Mus' be a whole damn army corps," growled another.

"Tain't nuff dust fo' many—sh-h-h."

The marchers were coming into sight now. In another second they would be in plain view of the hidden horsemen. They emerged from around the bend.

"Well, ah'll be damned!" muttered the first cavalryman to regain his breath.

"Sh-h-h! We'll grab 'em as they go pas'."

Eight Negro soldiers and their one prisoner tramped along, totally unaware of the patrol in ambush. The Negroes were chattering excitedly. The white man was sullen and kept pace only because he was prodded from behind, occasionally. A bloody rag around his arm indicated that he had not been captured without a struggle. His hands were tied behind him. The horsemen at the road-fork were poised for their coup. Captors and captive were only a few yards away now. On they came!

A sudden dash from the bushes! A flash of sabres! The Negroes were surrounded. They surrendered in terror. Their prisoner gave a yell of delight.

"Hush, you dern fool! You'll have the whole Yankee army down on us with that screechin'," exclaimed one of the cavalrymen. "Climb up heah behindst me. Turn 'round so's ah kin cut you loose."

"What you gonna do with these damn Niggers, Lars?" another inquired.

The one addressed as Lars, the leader of the patrol,

scratched his hairy chin and squinted a glintless eye. He was thinking. "Nigger soldiers!" he growled, as the tobacco juice exuded from the corners of his mouth. "A-shootin' at white men!"

"Ah reckon we cain't be takin' no prisoners, Lars."

Lars was still thinking. He glanced up at the sun.

"We got plen'y time," he concluded, still growling more to himself than to his companions. "Niggers a-shootin'!"

By now the patrol had herded their eight prisoners off the Pike and were back in hiding at the road-fork.

"You Niggers leave them muskets in the bushes an' git goin' up this heah road," ordered Lars. "Jemmie, you an' Bristoe ride on up ahaid. The Niggers will foller behindst yo' all, an' the rest o' us will bring up the rear."

The little caravan set out briskly along the narrow, country road in the direction of Bull Run Mountain—the white men in grey, riding—the black men in blue, walking. For nearly an hour they plodded along silently under the fury of the August sun. Then Lars gave an order. They turned off the road into a little valley, thickly covered on the slopes with strapping red oaks and white birches. The bed of a mountain stream, long since dried up in the summer heat, afforded easy access up the narrow valley. Two towering peaks, like silent sentinels, rose in their majesty on either side, to guard the sacredness and tranquility of the tiny vale between them.

The party halted out of sight of the roadway in a small clearing, completely screened by the twists and bends of the meandering stream-bed and the mass of underbrush that lined its banks.

Lars produced a rope from his saddle and threw it to the horseman nearest him.

"String 'em up," he said nonchalantly, nodding toward the nearest oak.

"You doan mean—," the soldier stammered.

"Ah mean jes what ah said—the Niggers, string 'em up," Lars repeated. "This heah's a white man's war, ah reckon."

The men in grey dismounted. Silently, they set about their grim task. There was only the one rope, so that progress was slow.

"Les shoot 'em, Lars," suggested one of the others.

"Cain't be no firin'," drawled Lars. "Git goin'."

The Negro prisoners were terrified. Some moaned in deep guttural tones. Others, rendered speechless with fright, followed with their panic-stricken eyes, every movement of their captors. Zeke began to pray in a low undertone. One of the others, whom Zeke had branded only a short time before as a doubting Thomas, found his tongue.

"Reckon yo' faith'll git us out dis mess, Zeke? Sho' got us in it," he twitted.

Zeke, down on his knees, ignored him and went on with his praying.

"How come, Zeke?" continued the other.

"Gib us faith, Lawd," wailed Zeke. "Gib us faith."

One by one the Negroes were bound, hung and then dropped to make way for the next. Three had already passed through this routine. Zeke was among the first to go. There were still five more. Lars and his men were hard at work.

"Throw up your arms!" rang out a clear, sharp command.

The gray men paused in their labors. A dozen men in blue with leveled muskets were looking down on Lars' party from the elevated bank of the dried stream.

There were still five more to be hung. Another rope was procured and the hanging proceeded. One by one the five white men in gray were laid beside the three black men in blue.

An Interview with Victor Daly

JAMES ROBERT PAYNE

Readers of *The Crisis* in the early 1930's saw a recurring advertisement for Victor Daly's *Not Only War*,[1] "At Last! The Negro Novel of the World War."[2] In addition to *Not Only War*, which remains a principal Afro-American fictionalization of Great War experience, Daly published three fine short stories, all in *The Crisis*, during the first half of the 1930's.[3] From his very first published story, "Private Walker Goes Patrolling," and on through his last fictional piece, "Still Five More," Daly's work is noteworthy for its consistently imaginative and innovative development of his primary theme, the Afro-American war experience.[4] In addition to his fiction, Daly has published a number of important articles on civil rights issues beginning with his 1920 essay on "The Housing Crisis in New York City."[5]

Upon entering government service with the United States Department of Labor during the first Roosevelt administration, Daly put aside fiction, and, after such an auspicious beginning, virtually disappeared from the literary scene. Yet of course Daly's important contributions remain for us. Although *Not Only War* has continued to attract critical attention from time to time,[6] full appreciation of the significance of Daly has been hampered by a severe lack of information about the author himself. In the course

This interview was first printed as "A *MELUS* Interview: Victor R. Daly" in *MELUS: The Journal of the Society for the Study of the Multi-Ethnic Literature of the United States* 12.2 (Summer 1985) and is reprinted with the permission of *MELUS*.

of work on a larger project I became determined to make
a breakthrough on the seeming information barrier surrounding Victor Daly. Working from a lead supplied by Dr.
Doris M. Hull of the Moorland-Spingarn Research Center
at Howard University, I discovered Daly to be still living
in Washington, D.C., and generously willing to respond to
an interview. After several initial telephone conversations,
Mr. Daly and I decided that it would be best if I prepared
some written questions for his responses in writing. My
edited version of the interview[7] which follows provides the
first significant published source of information on Daly's
life,[8] his beginnings as an author, and his views on writing.

INTERVIEWER: How did you get started writing?
DALY: I started writing in high school and won some con-
 tests promoted by the English or history classes. In
 1909 during my freshman year in high school the *New
 York Times* held a contest open to high school youth on
 the three hundredth anniversary of the discovery of the
 Hudson River as part of a Henry Hudson Festival. My
 version of the discovery won a bronze medal.
  During my sophomore year English class I wrote a
 report of two weeks of activities in the prior summer
 of a camp conducted by St. David's Church and won
 first prize. An interesting sidelight was the fact that the
 prize had been announced in advance as being a "bronze
 medal." But when the teacher saw that the winner was
 not one of the white students in the mostly white Morris High School he gave me a penny and told me that
 was my "bronze medal."
  During my junior year in high school the *New York
 Evening Globe* held a contest in which the high school
 contestants were to write a report on some athletic
 event in which all the city public high schools had been
 involved. As Captain of the Morris High School Cross
 Country Squad and a member of the Rifle Team, I attended many athletic events and my entry was selected

as the best one. During my senior year I wrote a weekly column for the *New York Evening Globe* on the athletic activities of all the public high schools in New York City.

I was president of the History Club in my senior year in high school which required some writing for the school paper. Primarily, however, the assignments for the president of the club were to speak at assemblies for special guests. This, of course, influenced my later confidence in making speeches of which there have been many.

My high school teachers encouraged me to study journalism in college, but I did not do so because I saw no opportunities then for Black journalists.

INTERVIEWER: What authors interested you and perhaps influenced you as you got started?

DALY: I read George A. Henty's books for boys during elementary school years. The stories about British soldiers had a lasting significance in my lifelong interest in all history. During high school I was known as a Civil War "buff." I read everything I could find time for on Generals Grant and Sherman, but do not remember by which authors. These probably had some nebulous influence—perhaps with my Civil War story "Still Five More," though not consciously.

INTERVIEWER: How did you regard writers associated with the Harlem Renaissance?

DALY: My writing was not influenced by any Black authors. During my last year of high school I heard about James Weldon Johnson and Alain Locke, but Black authors' work was not used in an all white high school. I met James Weldon Johnson when we lived in adjoining apartments in Harlem after World War I. I met Alain Locke after I moved to Washington, D.C.

INTERVIEWER: What other writers did you know and associate with, and how did their work influence yours?

DALY: After moving to Washington in 1922 and meeting

other persons interested in writing, I helped to establish the "Writers' Club" in the late twenties or early thirties, and I was an active member until it was disbanded in the fifties as the members aged or lost interest. Local Washington writers included: May Miller Sullivan, Georgia Johnson, Merze Tate, Isabel Lindsay, Arnett Lindsay, and J. Leon Langhorne, but none of these persons had an influence on the style or content of my writing.

INTERVIEWER: How does your war experience relate to your fiction?

DALY: "Private Walker Goes Patrolling" was based on a true incident reported to me by one of my first lieutenants on his return from a patrol with a German prisoner. The prisoner was actually captured with his pants down as he was using a latrine. The character of Jerry Walker, however, was fictional, although he was probably a composite of numerous types in the service.

"Goats, Wildcats and Buffalo" was a true incident in my own experience. The Germans knew all the time that our outfit was replacing the white soldiers. But they did not want to break the unwritten law of silence by bringing about unnecessary fighting when there was nothing to be gained but a small parcel of heavily wooded land.

INTERVIEWER: Does your Civil War story "Still Five More" relate to your own World War I experience? Do you have any recollections about this good story to pass on to readers and students of American literature?

DALY: "Still Five More" is my version of a true story told to me by an elderly Black man who lived on a plantation near Appomattox as a child during the Civil War. His father had been one of the members of the patrol.

I met him during the year 1922 when I worked for Dr. Carter Woodson, editor of the *Journal of Negro History*, and was on a history gathering mission to Appomattox with a friend who was a native son. Because of my interest in the Civil War, I gathered as much information as possible about Blacks during the Civil War period who were eye witnesses to incidents which occurred in Northern Virginia.

INTERVIEWER: In what respects is your novel *Not Only War* directly autobiographical?

DALY: The characters are fictional and the action is only partially autobiographical. Descriptions of places, especially the troop movement up the steep hill toward the end of the novel, are based on actual experiences which were fictionalized in hindsight.

INTERVIEWER: Is the college background of *Not Only War* based in any way on your own experience at Cornell? Did you base any of the Southern settings of *Not Only War* on any actual experiences which you might have had in the South?

DALY: Nothing at Cornell was like the novel. I had no experience in the South before writing it.

INTERVIEWER: Your characters Montgomery Jason and Robert Casper in Not Only War are so sharply drawn it is as if they were taken from life. Was there an officer who was the model for Casper? Is Jason someone you knew?

DALY: Jason and Casper are totally fictional.

INTERVIEWER: Do you have unpublished fiction or poetry?

DALY: No unpublished fiction or poetry.

INTERVIEWER: Could you tell me something about your non-fictional writing?

DALY: Beginning in 1920 with the publishing of the article on "The Housing Crisis in New York City" in the December issue of *The Crisis*, my writings were focused on race relations, segregation, labor union prejudices, lack of employment opportunities for non-white persons, particularly after I went to work for the Department of Labor in 1934. Some of these articles were published in *The Washington Post* and *The Star* newspapers in D.C. One of them, published originally in *The Washington Post*, was subsequently reprinted in *The Congressional Record*. I was presented with their Distinguished Service Award by the Department of Labor in 1956 in recognition of my work in effecting integration of Black personnel in the transportation system in D.C. In addition to the written articles, I made countless speeches on these same problems by invitation from high schools, colleges, and civic groups since I was the leading minority group expert in the Department of Labor.

I have articles in *The Journal of Intergroup Relations* (Summer 1961), *Employment Service Review* (October 1966), *Employment Security Review* (August 1956), and *The Crisis* (December 1920, May 1933, and June 1939).

INTERVIEWER: I am well aware of your longstanding interest in bridge. Could you tell me something about your activity in this area?

DALY: From the beginning of the organization of the American Bridge Association in 1932 I worked toward elimination of segregation in contract bridge circles. My efforts were finally successful in 1958 when the ABA held its Summer National Tournament at the Henry Hudson Hotel in New York City. Since then, the ABA has been welcome in first class hotels for their semi-annual National Tournaments, and local clubs have also used first class facilities regularly.

In a few cities the originally all white American Contract Bridge League allowed Black bridge players to participate in their games, and I was one of the first to play when in 1949 I was a partner of Albert Morehead, the liberal bridge columnist for the *New York Times*, in a tournament in Boston. But all ACBL Club doors did not open quickly, and I was rejected for local ACBL membership in the early 1960's. Subsequently, in 1964 after a long series of negotiations the ACBL bylaws were amended and some of the clubs accepted Black members. It was not until 1967, however, that the entire membership of the ACBL ratified its bylaws to permit non-white bridge players to join any local ACBL club and to play at any of their bridge tournaments.

INTERVIEWER: An entry in *Who's Who in the South and Southwest* (14th ed., 1975-76) is, to my knowledge, about the only biographical information available for you for students of American literature, an unfortunate situation, considering your significance as a principal Black fictionist of World War I. Could you expand on that bare bones Who's Who note so that students of American literature will have something to turn to?

DALY: Here is a brief summary of my life written for the American Bridge Association:

Victor Daly, at age six, was among the pioneers of black students in public education in New York City. He attended old P.S. 89 at the corner of 134th Street and Lenox Avenue in 1901, and was one among a handful of non-white children. The Dalys had moved from 25th Street and 9th Avenue, not far from the site of the old St. Phillips Episcopal Church. When big business and speculators began to buy huge tracts of choice properties in downtown Manhattan's West Side, the occupants were forced out. Some went to Brooklyn, some to Long Island, but the majority went north and settled in an area known as Harlem, which was just opening up to black people.

The Daly family followed the trend. Later they moved still farther north, settled in the Bronx, and Victor transferred to a fine school, P.S. 10. Although he was just a little shaver, about ten years of age, he attracted the attention of the teachers and the school principal, Evandor Childs. Mr. Childs was one of the most able and respected educators in the New York school system for whom a high school was named after his death. Mr. Childs had Victor read all school announcements at the school assemblies each week.

After graduation from P. S. 10 in 1911 Victor enrolled in Morris High School in the Bronx, one of the city's finest schools. He soon became known throughout

Morris, a school of some two thousand students where there were less than twenty black students during those years. He was a born athlete and very competitive. He became captain of the cross country team, was a mile runner on the track team, and found the time to be a star on Morris' crack rifle team, which won the New York State High School Championship for 1914 and 1915. He graduated with honors in 1915 with two academic scholarships to Cornell University, which he entered in the fall of 1915.

At the outbreak of World War I in 1917, he was sent to the Officers' Training Camp at Fort Des Moines, Iowa, commissioned a first lieutenant six months later, and assigned to the 367th Infantry, the famous "Buffaloes Regiment," at Camp Upton in Long Island. After serving for a year overseas, he finished his collegiate training, and joined the New York unit of the National Urban League. He moved to Washington, D.C., in 1922 as the business manager of Dr. Carter Woodson's *Journal of Negro History*. He was employed as an interviewer by the United States Department of Labor in 1934, and advanced through Personnel Officer, Fiscal Officer to Deputy Director of the United States Employment Service for the District of Columbia by the time he retired in 1966. He received the Department of Labor's top citation, the Distinguished Service Award, in 1956.

NOTES

1. *Not Only War: A Story of Two Great Conflicts* (1932; rpt. College Park, Md.: McGrath Publishing Co., 1969).

2. See for example *The Crisis*, 41 (January 1932), 469.

3. "Private Walker Goes Patrolling," *The Crisis*, 37 (June 1930), 199–201, 213; "Goats, Wildcats and Buffalo," *The Crisis*, 39 (March 1932), 91; "Still Five More," *The Crisis*, 41 (February 1934), 44–45.

4. I have work in progress which considers Daly's significance in American fiction.

5. *The Crisis*, 21 (December 1920), 61–62.

6. See especially Hugh M. Gloster, *Negro Voices in American Fiction* (Chapel Hill: The Univ. of North Carolina Press, 1948), pp. 217–218.

7. The original interview papers will ultimately be deposited at the Moorland-Spingarn Research Center, Howard University.

8. See also the short note on Daly in *Who's Who in the South and Southwest*, 14th ed. (1975-76), p. 159.